Ethan
and the
Seven
Chakras

Created by Yvette Farkas

Illustrated by Jana Rothwell

SINGING SOUL BOOKS

Ethan and the Seven Chakras (Book 1)
© 2024 by Yvette Farkas

All rights reserved. No part of this publication may be reproduced, distributed, or transmitted in any form or by any means, including photocopying, recording, or other electronic or mechanical methods, without the prior written permission of the publisher, except in the case of brief quotations for noncommercial uses permitted by copyright law.

Cover Illustration and Interior Design:
Jana Rothwell

Editing:
Poh Lin Cheng
Sherri Mellamed
Bella Jasper

ISBN:
Ethan and the Seven Chakras (Print book)
978-0-9866551-5-9
Ethan and the Seven Chakras (E-book)
978-0-9866551-6-6
Ethan and the Seven Chakras (Audiobook)
978-0-9866551-7-3

Published by:
Singing Soul Books
Website www.singingsoulbooks.com
Email info@singingsoulbooks.com

Disclaimer:
The techniques and tools presented in this book are intended for personal development and growth. While every effort has been made to ensure the accuracy and effectiveness of the information provided, the author and publisher assume no responsibility for any consequences resulting from the application of the methods described herein. Readers are advised to use their discretion and take personal responsibility for implementing these techniques. Personal development is a subjective journey, and individual results may vary based on personal circumstances, commitment, and application.

It is important to consult with relevant professionals or experts, where appropriate, before applying any of the suggestions in these books, especially if you have underlying health conditions or concerns. The author and publisher disclaim any liability, loss, or risk incurred directly or indirectly as a result of the use and application of the information presented in this book. Furthermore, readers are encouraged to approach personal development with an open mind and consider seeking additional resources, guidance, or support to complement the tools presented in this book. The author does not endorse any specific methodologies or approaches as the sole solution for everyone.

By reading this book, you acknowledge and agree that you are fully responsible for your own choices, actions, and outcomes. The author and publisher shall not be held liable for any damages, losses, or adverse consequences arising directly or indirectly from the information provided in this book.

Your personal development journey is uniquely yours, and this book serves as a guide rather than a definitive prescription. Embrace it with an open heart and a discerning mind.

Get all 8 books in the series:

Ethan and the Seven Chakras

Book 1: INTRODUCTION TO THE SEVEN CHAKRAS AND ETHAN
Get to know Ethan and the basics of the 7 main chakras as he overcomes his fear of public speaking.

Book 2: SAFELY CONNECTED TO EARTH
Learn to ground your Root Chakra with Ethan as he gets help for his grandfather after an unexpected accident and a scary hike to find his way home.

Book 3: FINDING YOUR PLACE IN THE TEAM
Balance your Sacral Chakra by becoming more comfortable in your skin with Ethan as he finds the courage to share his passions with others.

Book 4: FINDING YOUR OWN TRUE PATH
Learn to trust your gut instincts as Ethan strengthens his Solar Plexus Chakra by consciously changing his mindset and approaching his soccer team in a new way.

Book 5: THE WAY OF THE HEART
Get vulnerable and stay authentic with Ethan, who uses the wisdom of the Heart Chakra to help his cousin come to terms with a dying pet he loves dearly.

Book 6: THE POWER OF TRUTHFUL WORDS
Use the guidance of the Throat Chakra to honour your truth with Ethan despite severe pushback and deeply uncomfortable conversations with his best friend after a precious statue is accidentally broken.

Book 7: THE LIGHT OF OUR MINDS
Use the power of the Third Eye Chakra with Ethan as he learns to use his intuition to make an impossible decision that could end a beloved friendship.

Book 8: THE SINGING TREE OF LIFE
Journey into alternate dimensions and explore lucid dreaming with Ethan as he uses the expanded awareness of the Crown Chakra to understand how we are interconnected and meet his soon-to-be-born brother's Soul.

Readers love these books!

"I can count on one hand the amount of books I've read front to back in a day. These are so beautifully written, I can't wait for more to be released!"

~ Chantel Jameson-Farkas, Canada

"***Stunningly and beautifully written***, these are highly insightful books on the seven Chakras! I've heard the term Chakra before, but never connected it to the spine and its direct influence on one's body. I tried the breathing exercise and even began taking notes as I read through the books; there is so much useful information hidden in the stories!

On a personal level, the power of the chakras hit home as I began to make connections to my own life. The follow-up exercises made sense. From my personal experience in teaching children aged 9 to 11 years old, I believe that these books share very important life skills and should be included in school curriculums.

What you have created is very important, and frankly, for people of all ages. These books are fantastic, and I can see being a very important resource added to school libraries, both at the elementary and high school level."

~ Mark Desjardins, Canada

"***A beautiful, thoughtful, and magical journey*** to exploring chakras. Embarking on a spiritual path feels inspiring, achievable, and understandable after reading these books. This is my type of education – fun and enriching to the soul! Truly a must-read for children, but arguably an essential read for all adults as well."

~ Poh, Canada

"***I am beyond amazed*** at the talent and genuine beauty and creativity in these books! I learned so much about planting! I will be the first to order many books as this story will be legendary and already is in my world. Thank you and bless your heart for the information that you will pass on to kids and adults. May this help to impact the world in a beautiful way."

~ Mel Kiss, The Dominican Republic

A message from Yvette:

Thank you to all the healers, teachers, mentors, guides, family, and friends who have nourished my spirit and inspired growth. I have so much appreciation and love for you all!

Thank you to my nephews, Ethan and Lukas, who inspired this book series with their thoughtful questions during our many forays into the woods, countless hours in grandma's garden, the cabin, and bee yard, during our early mornings foraging for herbs, time spent lying in the thick, green moss watching the clouds float by and chatting, and of course, reading wonderful, uplifting stories each night after our meditations. It was great fun creating these stories based on many of our family adventures together, conversations, and heartfelt questions about some of life's mysteries.

My dear family, we have created and enjoyed many wonderful memories and moments together; my heart is filled with love, admiration, and gratitude for all we have shared. Thank you for supporting me in so many ways. I am very grateful to each and every one of you: Anyu, Apu, Otti, Attila, Katimama, Chantel, Nicole, Ethan, Lukas, Björn, Hudson, Bennett, Rollo, Gyuri, George, Ernestine, and our family dogs; Zserbo, Lui, Jake, and Moose.

Jutka, Misi, and Robi; I place you in the family category as that is what you are to me. Thank you for your neverending support and excitement about my various projects and adventures over the years. I feel blessed to have grown up with you in my life.

Carla Roter, I've had the pleasure and privilege of benefiting from your wisdom, love, support, and kindness for decades. Your unwavering belief in me and encouragement towards my dreams have meant the world. Through you, I've gained invaluable insights into compassion, witnessing firsthand how it can look when opening oneself to greater love and practicing non-judgment amidst life's challenges and triggers. Your constant support and presence have been a true blessing, profoundly impacting my life for the better. I've grown and learned immensely under your gentle guidance, through our honest conversations, and by observing your own graceful navigation through life's myriad "human moments." Thank you, dearest Kapha Mama.

Marcel; you bring so much joy, laughter, and inspiration to my life. You are one of those rare Souls who has the great capacity to hold a sacred space of incredible strength for me to relax into, supporting and empowering me to be my best and shine my light with the world from that space - a space of deep grounding, respect, care, appreciation, fun, and resilience. I love that you inspire me (and many others) with your own examples of growth and consistently strive for personal greatness. Thank you for being on this journey with me and for gently encouraging me to keep going and do what is important to my heart and Soul. I'm so glad you were "persistent." I feel blessed and excited to co-create this beautiful life with you.

Tom and Lilou, you have enriched my life with your shining Spirits, intelligence, humour, and sense of play. It excites me to see what your next amazing chapter of life will look like, and what beautiful gifts you will continue to bring to the world. Thank you for welcoming me into yours.

Deep appreciation and acknowledgement to all the guides who transmitted key information to be added to these books through dreams, visions, and synchronicities. The intent to have this uplift and empower its readers was obvious. This book series was a beautiful, collaborative co-creation between many that was joyful, easy, and flowed with love, wisdom, and clarity. I am honoured to have been a part of its transmission and excited to share it with humanity.

Jana, working with you in this creative playground has been an absolute pleasure. Your beautiful and clear energy, extensive professional experience, and incredible talent has elevated these books to new levels. What you have created is sheer magic and it excites me to know that many will have the benefit of enjoying your wonderful paintings and illustrations. You have brought many new ideas to the project and assisted in ensuring all the different pieces work synergistically well together. Deep gratitude to you for all that you are and all that you have brought and continue to share with the world. It has been an honour to take this path with you.

Thank you to my incredible writing partner, Wayne Bloemhof. You were the gift the Universe delivered when I made my request for assistance with this Soul project. Your ability to tune in to this vision, feel and deliver its essence, and work in harmony with me (and all our guides) was amazing. It was effortless and fun working with you. I am deeply grateful to you Wayne. You helped give these stories legs on which to stand. You truly are the "unofficial wordsmith for the River of Life," as you often say.

A big thank you to Juliana D'Costa who helped start the process of coming up with and creating the illustrations for these books. The countless hours spent laughing together, working in focused silence, and feeding off of each other's creative and "happy heart" energy was incredibly special. You provided so much positivity, clarity, and guidance that helped move this project forward. I love the frog illustrations - and all the others you did. You are incredibly talented my friend. All the good energy you have put into these books will be felt by its countless readers. What a special gift from you.

Thank you to my incredible user testing group. You read and re-read these books, providing valuable feedback, helping to ensure the information being shared made sense no matter the age or background knowledge of the reader. Your honesty and insight have made these books all the more easily received because you cared enough to dive deep into them, noticing loose ends that needed tying.

Sherri Mellamed      Juliana D'Costa
Poh Lin Cheng   Mark Desjardins
Shiren VanCooten   Maria Kiss
Nikolet Gárdián   Milena Gosevski
Éva Csuka   Carla Roter

Sincere gratitude to my outstanding editors; Poh Lin Cheng, Sherri Mellamed, and Bella Jasper. It was after your edits that I felt good about releasing this work to the world. The time you spent going through these books shows in the quality and final product. Thank you for helping to birth this inspired work with clarity and sincerity.

Hi everyone, I'm Ethan.

My aunt Yvette wrote some pretty awesome books about our family adventures. You'll like them.

My favourite book is the third one; in it, I am a bee who learns about "bee-things" and how to overcome self-doubt. That's something I've had to learn to do in real life too. I bet you can relate.

I'm the main character in these books, but you'll also get to meet my brothers, parents, and other family members. To help you remember who everyone is, I've drawn a picture for you. I like to keep things simple, so I made it a stick figure portrait.

I think kids and adults will all like these books. They feel good to read or have read to you, and you learn a lot of fascinating facts about things like using posture and breathing to help you feel more confident in life.

I hope you enjoy our family books!

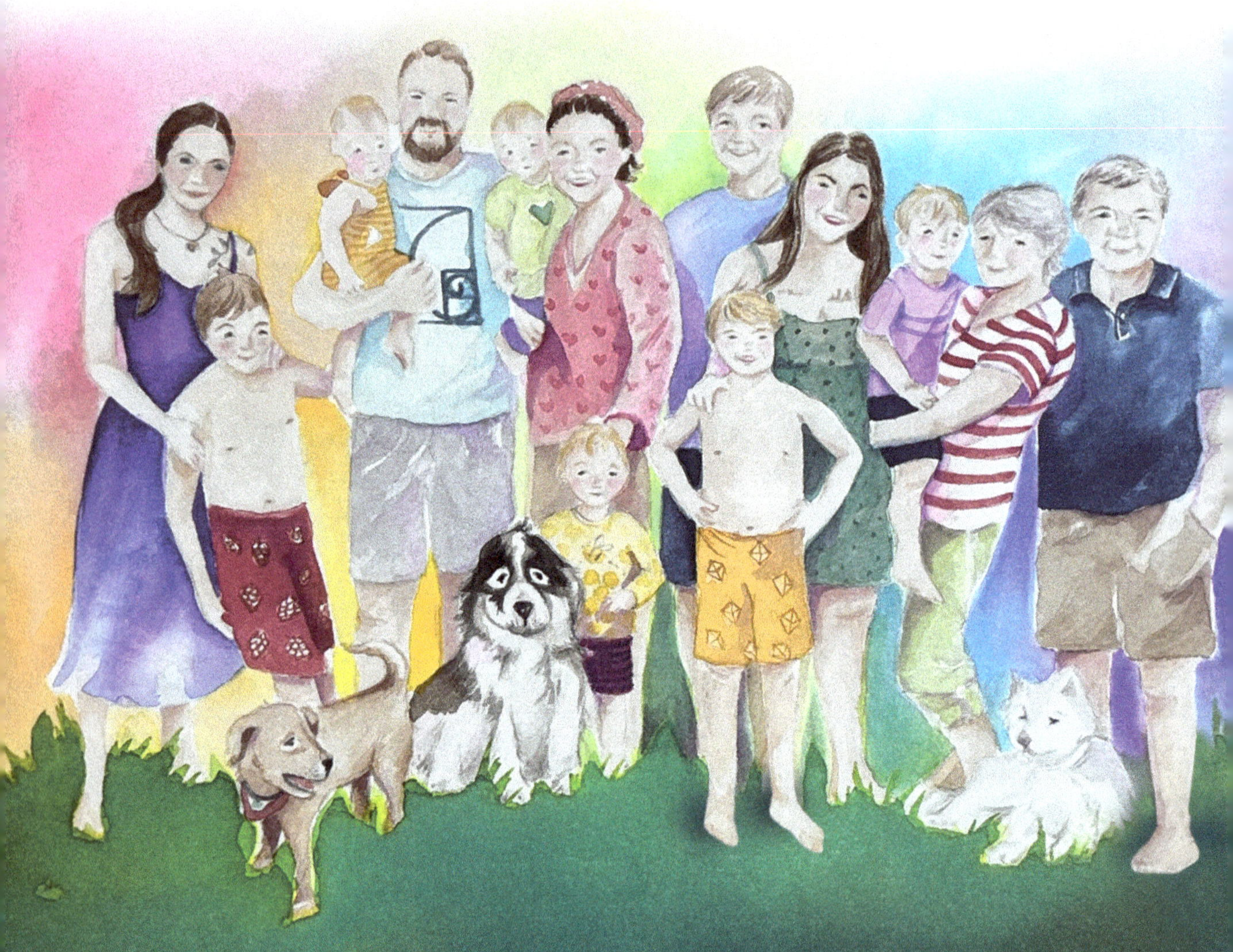

Aunt Yvette with Ethan, Lui (dog), Uncle Attila with baby Bennett,
Moose (dog), Aunt Nicole with baby Rollo and Björn, Ethan's Dad (Tom),
Ethan's Mom (Chantel) with Lukas, Grandma Suzan with Hudson,
Grandpa Otto, Jake (dog)

Welcome to Your Journey of Heart and Brain Harmony!

Dear friend, before we dive into the enchanting world of Ethan's story, let's embark on a special mission—one that involves the magic within you!

Take a Deep Breath

Close your eyes, take a big, deep breath in through your nose, feeling your chest expand like a balloon. Now, slowly exhale through your nose. Repeat this a couple of times, and notice how it makes you feel calm and centered.

Heartbeat Connection

Place your hand over your heart. Can you feel its gentle rhythm? As you slowly inhale and exhale, imagine sending love and kindness to your heart. Feel it glow with warmth.

Feel the Vibes

Smile as you imagine something or someone that helps you feel the warm hug of care, the loving touch of compassion, the upliftment of appreciation, and the cozy blanket of gratitude.

* **Care**
* **Compassion**
* **Appreciation**
* **Gratitude**

Let those feelings dance in your heart, creating a warmth that spreads throughout your body. Keep breathing slowly and deeply.

Empowerment Words

As you read this book, carry these potent words with you - "I am loved, I am appreciated, I am valued, I am cherished, I am smart, I am important, I am capable, I am confident, I am worthy, I am enough, and my heart holds incredible power." Whisper them when you need a boost of courage or a dose of self-compassion.

Smile and close your eyes again as you take another deep breath, feeling warm, loving energy permeate your body, soothing and relaxing you completely.

Wishing you an edifying journey filled with discovery and joy.

Crown Chakra
Third Eye Chakra
Throat Chakra
Heart Chakra
Solar Plexus Chakra
Sacral Chakra
Root Chakra

Note to parents and readers:

This is an introduction to the concept of chakras (pronounced "cha" as in "charge" and "kra."). It shows different ways of interpreting and approaching situations depending on what lens - or chakra - you are looking through. It contains many seeds of knowledge hidden "in plain sight" throughout the stories. When watered, these seeds will empower readers to intuitively guide themselves towards a deeper understanding and awakening of their own innate wisdom and potential.

The questions at the end of each section are designed to inspire meaningful conversation between you, dear readers and listeners. Use this opportunity to engage in thoughtful, heart-to-heart conversations, bringing you closer to one another as you make insightful connections.

Ethan and the Seven Chakras
Introduction to the Seven Chakras and Ethan (Book 1)

Chapter 1: New in Town.. 15

Chapter 2: A Strange Dream... 18

Chapter 3: The First Chakra.. 21

Chapter 4: Getting Along With Others........................... 27

Chapter 5: The Second Chakra....................................... 30

Chapter 6: Feeling Sorry For Yourself.......................... 34

Chapter 7: The Third Chakra... 36

Chapter 8: The Power of Love... 42

Chapter 9: The Fourth Chakra.. 47

Chapter 10: Speaking Your Truth................................... 53

Chapter 11: The Fifth Chakra.. 55

Chapter 12: In the Mind's Eye.. 59

Chapter 13: The Sixth Chakra... 61

Chapter 14: The End of the Week................................... 66

Chapter 15: The Seventh Chakra.................................... 68

Chapter 16: Coming Home... 72

Chapter 1: New in Town

Ethan and his family lived in the only red house in the whole neighbourhood.

Not only did Ethan live in a house that was a little different, he was a little different too. You see, Ethan's family had just moved to town, and Ethan was new at school. Unlike most kids, however, Ethan and his folks travelled all over the world before they came here.

Ethan's dad was a marine mechanic who fixed boats and all kinds of engines. His mom was a talented designer who made beautiful furniture and art for people. They both loved working with their hands and frequently created projects together as a family. This year, they planned on building a jungle gym in the backyard made from recycled wood. Ethan's parents had drawn up the plans after hearing what the kids would most enjoy doing outside. Once they returned from their trip, they would get the kids together and start building it. There would be a climbing wall, obstacle course, balance beams, zipline, and slackline. It was going to be awesome!

Even though he was still a kid, Ethan had already lived in five countries. He had friends in Morocco, Turkey, China, and Hungary. Now, he was back in Canada.

Ethan was ten years old, tall, and slender, with brown hair and eyes and freckles across the top of his nose and cheeks. He was smart, told funny jokes, and enjoyed cooking. He was a very curious and thoughtful kid, always asking questions and trying to figure things out. He wasn't afraid to talk with adults and often had long conversations with them. However, he felt shy around other kids. It was as if they couldn't quite understand him sometimes. He also felt a little nervous about trying new things, but that's pretty normal; even adults get nervous at times.

School had just started, and next week was going to be Ethan's big chance to make new friends. It would be his turn to speak in front of the class. Each day, a new student got to tell the class about their family and share stories about their life. Ethan decided he was going to tell the class about his world travels. He thought his classmates would be impressed with his stories, and this would help him make new friends.

As it turned out, though, things don't always work out exactly the way we think they will. Ethan's parents were away for a whole week, and last night, they called to say they might be away even longer. This disappointed Ethan, as he wanted to work on this class project with his parents. His grandmother was looking after him and his brothers while they were away. Although she could have helped him with his project, Ethan decided not to ask her for help. Even though he loved his grandmother, she was old-fashioned and wasn't great at using the computer. Worst of all, Ethan was beginning to feel worried about his upcoming speech. In fact, he felt as if he was getting sick.

What if nobody liked his stories? What if nobody wanted to be his friend? What if mom and dad didn't come back for a whole month? How was he going to survive an entire week with Grandma Suzan and her old-fashioned ideas of "fun", such as reading and gardening, instead of letting him play his video games?

Just as he was thinking this, he looked out of his window and saw something he hadn't noticed before. Across the road from Ethan's red house was another brightly painted house—a green house. Like Ethan's, it was a little different too. Ethan wondered if the people that lived in it were also different.

As it turned out, that green house was the home of another family very similar to Ethan's.

Chapter 2: A Strange Dream

Priya was a cheerful girl who lived in the bright green house across the road. She was in the same class as Ethan at school. She had beautiful black hair that reached down her back, brown eyes that always seemed to twinkle when she smiled, and a calmness about her. She was relaxed and cheerful most of the time. Ethan noticed that she never seemed to rush about as most other kids. She took her time and still managed to get all her schoolwork done by the end of class.

That day, she came over with her mom, and they offered to help Ethan catch up with his schoolwork. Since Ethan hadn't started school until October, he had missed quite a lot. Priya's mom chatted with Grandma Suzan and Ethan's younger brothers, Lukas and Hudson, while Ethan and Priya sat at a table with their books.

At first, it was awkward because they were both quite shy. However, they were stuck there while everyone else talked in the other room, so they soon started talking too. Ethan decided to tell Priya about the strange dream he had the night before.

In his dream, he saw a spinning red wheel at the bottom of a tree, near the roots. There was a dream guide too. The guide was a monkey that could fly! The flying monkey guide showed Ethan all kinds of things about that big red wheel. Ethan couldn't remember all of it, and he didn't know what it meant.

He did remember that the dream was also about planet Earth and all the fascinating and wonderful creatures on it. First, the monkey guide showed Ethan the ground—the sand and rocks under our feet. Then, he showed him many kinds of plants and animals on Earth. In the dream, the flying monkey showed Ethan how all kinds of creatures belonged in families.

There were bug families, plant families, flocks of birds, and schools of different kinds of fish. In fact, all living things were like one big, giant family! All of us belong here together. Each part of life is special, sacred, and important—even the dirty dirt!

"This whole planet is one big, bright, beautiful home," the monkey guide laughed, "and everyone is a distant relative of everyone else. Even the mountains and the sky are second cousins, twice removed."

Ethan told Priya about the funny dream, and then, she told him the strangest thing:

"What you are describing from your dream sounds like some of the things my mom talks about. She teaches yoga and meditation after school. Have you ever heard of a chakra before?"

Ethan didn't know what a chakra was, so Priya explained: There are different types of energies in and around our bodies. When the energy is flowing, we feel good and healthy. When the energy is blocked somewhere, we can feel unbalanced or unwell. A chakra is like a spinning wheel of energy that is invisible and acts like a portal. A 'portal' is a doorway. In your body, you have different kinds of 'doors'; for example, your mouth, eyes, and ears. The chakras are energetic doors or portals. It is an energetic map that shows what you like and don't like and where you feel stuck. It also helps us figure out how to get unstuck.

You have seven main chakras. There are many more, but the seven main ones in your body are special. Each chakra is connected to a different part of life. If your chakras are healthy, then life feels good. If they are out of balance, you can get sick, tired, angry, or sad—and things seem to go wrong.

Ethan still wasn't sure he understood, but he nodded and decided to ask more questions after their schoolwork was done.

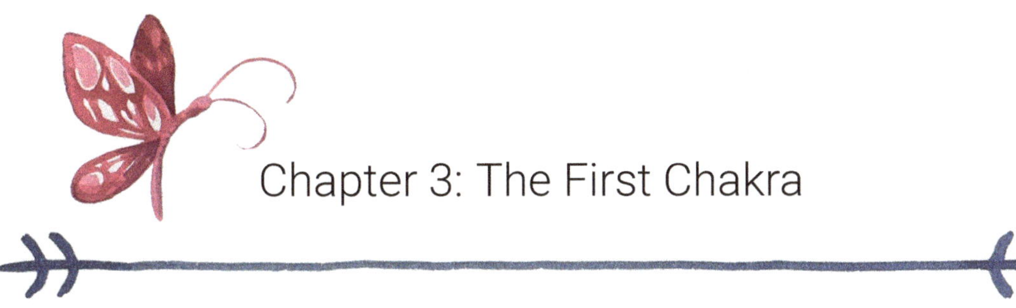

Chapter 3: The First Chakra

That evening, Ethan, his brothers, and Grandma Suzan were invited over for dinner with Priya's family. Ethan was very hungry as he had been working hard all afternoon on his school project. They ate traditional Indian food with delicious naan bread. It was spicy and wonderful! There was a big plate in the middle with many smaller bowls on it, each containing a different food item. There were all kinds of interesting and colourful dishes, and everyone shared. Ethan felt satiated, comfortably full, and completely relaxed after their meal. He was no longer hungry and could now focus on their conversation. Before he got into his story, he thanked Priya's parents for the delicious meal. Priya's mom noticed Ethan's good manners and appreciated his polite words of thanks.

"It's so quiet without a TV, computer, or music playing in the background," observed Ethan.

"You are quite right, Ethan. We enjoy our food and each other's company more without distractions," replied Priya's mom as she sipped a cup of lemon water and smiled at him.

"That's how we eat mindfully, by being present, chewing our food well, enjoying the flavours in each bite, and feeling appreciation for all the blessings in our lives. It's also special to be able to eat together; not every family is able to do that."

Ethan nodded silently. He was thinking about his parents eating by themselves, without him and his brothers and wondered if they missed them.

"My aunt often tells us to chew our food well, too," mused Ethan.

"She's right," smiled Priya's mom.

"Tell me, kids, do you know where your saliva comes from?"

The kids looked at her with wide eyes, neither one knowing the answer.

"There are three kinds of salivary glands in different areas of your mouth that squirt out saliva when you need it," replied Priya's mom, Ambika.

"When you think about eating, your body instantly begins preparing to digest the food you are thinking about—even before you put the food into your mouth. In this way, we could say that digestion begins in the mind."

"Do you ever count the number of times you chew?" Grandma Suzan asked the kids.

Now, they really looked surprised!

"Uh, no," began Lukas, "should we?"

"Try it the next time you eat. Chew your food at least 36 times. If the food in your mouth is completely liquefied, and you've mixed a lot of saliva with it, go ahead and swallow. If there are still little bits of food in your mouth, then keep chewing until there are no more pieces. Chewing your food well helps your body to digest it smoothly without using up a lot of your energy," explained Grandma Suzan.

"That's exactly right," smiled Priya's mom.

"Once you get used to chewing until all your food is a liquid before swallowing, you don't need to keep counting how many times you chew. It's a tool used to keep you focused and help you remember to chew well since most people forget to eat with awareness." Priya's mom explained further.

"I know it's important to eat healthy food, but I had no idea that how you eat is just as important," exclaimed Ethan.

After the meal, they all sat around the table, talking and getting to know each other. Ethan spoke about the monkey guide and the red wheel from his dream.

"Interesting! Your dream was all about the first chakra." Priya's mom said.

She went on to explain:

The seven main chakras are found in a line near a person's backbone—the spine. The first chakra is near the bottom of your spine—called the 'base or root'. The seventh one is right at the top of your head, called the 'crown chakra'. There are other chakras too, but these are the seven main ones people must understand and master first.

She explained that the red wheel from his dream sounded just like the first chakra, near the roots. The first chakra is about feeling safe in the world, feeling secure about basic needs and survival, and understanding how to create healthy boundaries. It's also about our connection to the Earth, our food, our physical home, and our family.

It's called the 'root chakra'. When the chakra is not working right and it's imbalanced, we may feel scared or worried. We might feel like something might harm us, or take something from us. We may feel lonely, disconnected, ungrounded, or unsafe. It's how you feel when things are uncertain and up in the air. That's why it's important to stay grounded.

Priya's mom added: "Don't misunderstand, Ethan. Being 'grounded' doesn't mean being sent to your room because you misbehaved. It means that you live naturally, in a way that helps you feel safe and comfortable. Your thoughts are in the present moment, not in the past or the future. Walking barefoot on the Earth, getting your hands into the soil by growing your own herbs and vegetables, climbing trees, spending time in the forest, swimming in a lake, and playing outside in nature to feel connected to Mother Earth all help to ground you in your body and feel deeply connected and in the present."

"Feeling grounded also means that you're down-to-earth and real. You can be yourself and know that you are enough because you are a divine spirit who is perfect, important, and loved."

"Being yourself takes courage and honesty, doesn't it? It's easier to do that when you feel safe, good in your skin, and happy with who you are. When you feel like that, then you know your first chakra is feeling good."

"When the first chakra is open and healthy, we feel connected to Mother Earth, like our own mother, and we feel safe."

"When the first chakra gets out of balance, we can feel too anxious to explore or try new things. When you don't feel safe, it's not a time to create or rest. It's a time to be vigilant and cautious."

"Oftentimes, when people have indigestion or their stomachs hurt, it's because their first chakra is out of balance. All their nervous energy goes to their stomach, making them feel queasy. When we don't feel like we belong, or think that no one likes us, or think that someone is upset with us, it can create an uneasy, heavy feeling in the pit of our stomach."

"It's not your fault or bad if this happens. It's a sign that you have been feeling a little nervous or uncomfortable about something. That's ok. Everyone gets uncomfortable sometimes. Even adults. Even your parents. The important thing is to acknowledge the feeling, figure out why you feel that way, and think about what you need to feel safe and comfortable again. It can also help to talk about it with your parents or to draw it out on paper."

"The good news is that you can change how you feel when you know how to balance your chakras."

"I sometimes feel queasy in my stomach," remarked Ethan, "especially when I have to get up in front of the class and give a speech, or do something that makes me really nervous."

Root Chakra Discussion Questions

1. How do you feel when you are playing outside in nature, close to trees, sunshine, and water? Does it feel better than being inside?

2. Do you enjoy building things with your hands? What do you like to make?

3. How do you feel about your own amazing body? Do you love every part of yourself? Are there any parts you don't like?

4. Do you like playing in the dirt or soil? Have you ever planted seeds and watched them grow?

5. What are some things that make you feel scared or nervous?

6. What helps you feel better when you are scared?

7. Have you ever had a stomach ache? If yes, why do you think you felt sick? Were you nervous about something?

8. Have you ever been away from your parents? Did you miss your family? What made you feel better? What things can you do to feel better next time?

9. Have you ever felt as if you are all alone or that no one understands you?

10. Have you ever felt unsafe somewhere or with someone?

11. Have you ever felt really hungry? What exactly did you feel in your body?

12. How do you feel after you've eaten delicious, nourishing food? Is you mood or energy level different?

13. How can you tell the difference between hunger and thirst?

14. Imagine moving to a new country with your family; what do you think that would be like?

15. Ask your parents these same questions.

Chapter 4: Getting Along with Others

The next day, it rained non-stop. Ethan sat by the window and stared out at the dreary puddles of water forming in the street. He felt bored and restless. He also felt very lonely.

He thought about his friends, so very far away, and wondered what they were doing. He thought about his mom and dad and wished they would come back early. He closed his eyes and imagined his mom's shiny brown hair and big brown eyes as she hugged him, smelling really good. He then thought about how much he enjoyed hanging out with his dad in his shop, helping him fix engines and laughing at all his dad jokes—even the ones that weren't too funny.

He thought about his Grandma Suzan, with her long silver hair piled up into a neat bun above her head, her kind eyes, her happy smile, and her witty comments. She was sharp and always knew when Ethan was up to something; when he needed a hug or had an exciting story to share, she was ready to listen. Grandma Suzan made many delicious meals for the family and told them curious stories about her childhood village in Hungary. Ethan usually enjoyed spending time with her, but today, he was feeling down.

That was precisely when a pleasant smell drifted into the room.

Ethan went into the kitchen to investigate. Grandma was making pancake batter! It was a special type of Hungarian pancake called "palachinta"— very thin and stuffed with jam, sweetened ground walnuts, chocolate, cinnamon, or lemony cottage cheese. He loved palachinta!

Even if Grandma Suzan didn't know how to use the computer very well, she knew how to cheer him up and make the best breakfast! For the first time today, Ethan was really happy that she was visiting. He felt deeply appreciative for everything she did for them. He walked right up to her and gave her a big hug, telling her how much he loved her. Grandma loved him too, very much.

She smiled and told Ethan to run across the road and invite Priya to join them for Hungarian-style pancakes with maple syrup and fruit.

Ethan flew out of the kitchen and ran all the way to Priya's green house.

Ethan's brothers, Lukas and Hudson were still sleeping, so Grandma Suzan made sure to save some palachinta for them to eat later.

Ethan and Priya got back just as Grandma Suzan was pouring the last of the batter into the pan. Soon after, the three of them were putting their favourite toppings into their palachinta and rolling them up. Ethan had apricot jam sprinkled with chocolate; Priya decided to try the sweet walnut while grandma made herself lemony cottage cheese palachinta. One of the many delightful things about living in Canada is the maple syrup—something all three of them liked. Ethan and Priya added a little maple syrup to their breakfast while grandma made them all a pot of peppermint tea fresh from the mint she grew in her garden.

They had a lot of fun, eating, licking their fingers, and laughing together. Suddenly, Ethan didn't feel so lonely after all—Priya was his first new friend in town—and even the rain didn't bother him so much anymore. He felt better and better, in fact. The more relaxed, loved, accepted, and nourished he felt, the more grounded he became. His first chakra was feeling better too. It had become rooted, grounded, and strong.

He asked Priya to tell him more about the chakras, and so, she started to explain all about the second chakra.

Infinity Symbol

Chapter 5: The Second Chakra

Priya finished chewing her last bite of palachinta and began to talk about the second chakra.

"Its colour is orange. It's called the 'Sacral chakra', and just like the first one, it acts like a portal connecting us to a part of life, the part that has to do with creativity, relationships, and pleasure—things that feel good."

"It sits about three inches below your navel in the center of your belly." Priya put her hand on her tummy, just below her belly button to show Ethan.

Grandma Suzan smiled as she continued the explanation. She also knew a little something about chakras, to Ethan's amazement.

"A lot of our energy is stored in that place, and so, the belly is where we feel some of our strongest emotions. That's what we call our gut feeling, and it helps us make good decisions. It's important to acknowledge those feelings, work through them, and find ways to resolve challenges instead of getting stuck in those feelings. We always know when something feels wrong, and we know when something feels right. Your gut feelings will tell you instantly if something is right or wrong for you. Always listen to your gut feelings. This is a part of your guidance system and it's connected to your emotions. Your feelings are powerful tools that help guide you in life."

Both Priya and Ethan nodded in acknowledgement.

Grandma Suzan got up to bring them another jar of apricot jam while speaking, "the first chakra reminds us that we are all connected to a giant family. When it is balanced, we feel safe and grounded. The second chakra is more personal; it connects us to our feelings, creativity, and imagination. Many of our choices have to do with feeling good. For example, when you think about food from the level of the first chakra, you eat it because you are hungry and need nourishment. At the level of the second chakra, you eat for the pleasure of it because the food tastes delicious, and you want to enjoy eating it."

"Do you understand the difference?" asked Grandma Suzan.

"Yes," replied Ethan as he made another roll of palachinta for himself. "I'm eating because palachinta tastes delicious, and I love it. So, my second chakra must be feeling good right now."

"Exactly," replied Grandma Suzan as she ate her last piece.

"The universe is incredibly creative," said Grandma Suzan admiringly. "In all of creation, nothing looks exactly alike. No two trees are exactly the same. No two leaves are exactly the same. No two snowflakes are exactly the same. Yet every single piece fits together perfectly and works in harmony with each other when in balance."

The three of them began to clear the table of dishes. Grandma Suzan washed while Priya and Ethan dried. She handed Priya a saucer and continued, "when your second chakra is happy and feeling good, you are creative; you can easily imagine all kinds of stories and solutions to problems. You know exactly how you feel about things, and you enjoy doing things like eating, dancing, singing, drawing, or playing for the sheer enjoyment of it—because it's fun and it feels good."

"When your second chakra is balanced, you feel positive and creative—ready to be yourself and enjoy connecting with others. When it is out of balance, you can feel bored, uninspired, uncomfortable with people, and cautious in your relationships."

Ethan took one of the freshly washed mugs from grandma's hands and asked, "is that why we want to play with others and spend time doing fun things with them when we feel good?"

"That would certainly show a healthy and happy second chakra," nodded Grandma Suzan.

"Speaking of relationships, there is one that is especially important, maybe even the most important one. Kids, can you think of who it's with?" Asked Grandma Suzan as they finished cleaning the kitchen.

After several attempts to guess, grandma finally revealed the answer.

"Darlings, the answer is you. The relationship you have with yourself is very special. Be loving and kind to yourself always. Speak encouragingly to yourself. Your spirit will thrive when you believe in yourself and feed it support and encouragement. Remember that."

Sacral Chakra Discussion Questions

1. What do you most enjoy eating?

2. How do you feel when you eat something delicious? Do you feel good in your body? Satiated? Satisfied? Do you also feel good in your mind?

3. What do you think it means to feel good in your mind?

4. What makes food delicious for you? The taste, the smell, the experience of eating together with your family, or something else?

5. What is your favourite way to play and have fun?

6. What are some things that make you special and a little different from others?

7. Do you ever feel lonely? When? Why do you think you may feel that way?

8. How can people shift feelings of being lonely to feelings of joy and happiness?

9. Do you have a hobby, craft, or activity that you enjoy?

10. What kinds of things do you like to create?

11. What kinds of people do you have relationships with? Friends, family, teachers, or other people?

12. Who are the important people in your life? Why are they important to you?

13. How do those people make you feel?

14. How are you important to your parents?

15. How are you important to your friends?

16. How do you like to connect with people? Do you prefer to play together, have conversations, explore new activities together, or do something else?

17. Do you know that you are a blessing, that you are special and loved, and here for a reason?

18. What talents and personal gifts do you enjoy sharing with the world?

19. What would you like your parents to know about you that they don't already know?

20. Ask your parents these same questions.

Chapter 6: Feeling Sorry For Yourself

The next day was a school day, but the rain continued. When Ethan got home, he looked miserable. He was feeling terribly sorry for himself.

"Why the long face, my handsome little grandson?" asked Grandma Suzan. She could tell right away that Ethan was unhappy.

"No reason! It's raining, and I'm bored. I want to do fun things, but there's nothing to do," complained Ethan.

"Hmm, are you sure that's the reason you seem so agitated and unhappy, or did something happen at school?" asked Grandma Suzan gently.

Ethan sat down and sighed a big sigh. He really seemed dejected.

"Tell me what happened," encouraged Grandma Suzan as she sat down next to him and put her arm around his shoulders.

Finally, he opened up and told Grandma Suzan that a girl at school had given her speech in front of the class. She spoke about foreign countries, and everyone in class loved it. Everyone, that is, except for Ethan—because the topic about foreign countries was supposed to be his thing!

Even worse, the constant rain meant that Ethan couldn't go to the park or play any of the fun outdoor activities he usually enjoyed.

"I think you're getting cabin fever," said Grandma Suzan. "That happens when you've been inside for too long and have a lot of pent-up energy. It's a good time to redirect it. What you need is some exercise to move that blocked energy—to move your body, your breath, and shift your attention. Doesn't Priya's mom teach a yoga class across the road? Why don't you join her today?"

Even though Ethan wasn't in the mood, he decided to go just to get out of the house. He had never been to a class before, and it turned out to be loads of fun. The class he joined was all about asanas, which are yoga poses. Everyone was doing poses with names like the 'lion' pose, the 'cobra' pose, and the 'sun salutation', which is a series of movements you do in combination with an inhalation, exhalation, or holding your breath. It sounds complicated, but after a few rounds, you really get into the swing of things and feel completely recharged.

Priya's mom said that Ethan did really well. "Keep practicing," she said, "it will keep you strong and healthy."

After the yoga class, Ethan wanted to know more about the chakras; how many were there again? Six? Or was it seven? So, Priya's mom told him more.

Chapter 7: The Third Chakra

Priya's mom, Ambika, and Ethan started to walk toward the garden at the front of the house where some of the other students were sipping a cup of jasmine green tea.

"Yellow is the colour of the sun, and yellow is the colour of the third chakra, also known as the 'Solar Plexus chakra'. Did you know that the word 'solar' means sun, Ethan?"

"I do now," smiled Ethan as they found a nice spot to sit next to a beautiful, tall maple tree with bright, yellow and orange leaves.

Priya's mom continued, "the third chakra sits in a special place in your body called the 'solar plexus.' That intriguing word, 'solar plexus,' means 'a network.' It's one of the reasons sunshine is so good for people. It elevates your mood, helps you to feel happy, and stimulates your body to make Vitamin D."

Ethan looked up as a gust of wind rustled the colourful leaves in the tall branches, sending a yellow leaf gently cascading down next to his leg. He picked it up, turned it over and said to Ambika, "this yellow leaf reminds me of the third chakra."

"Me too," smiled Priya's mom in reply, then explained, "there is a spot near the middle of your body about halfway above your belly button and where your ribs join at the front of your chest. Right there, in that sensitive hollow space near your spine is your solar plexus," she said and pointed to it on her body by placing her open palm above her solar plexus chakra.

"Ethan, can you find it on your body?" She asked.

"Is it here?" inquired Ethan as he gently pressed down on that same hollow spot he had seen Priya's mom point out.

"Yes, that's exactly right, Ethan," she said as she nodded.

"This is where our third chakra resides. It is all about who we are and how we feel about ourselves. It is about your personal power and your ability to exert influence in the world. Do you feel good about yourself most of the time? Do you feel that your parents, teachers, and friends are proud of you and care about you? Do you have goals you've accomplished that made you feel validated? Are there challenges you've overcome that helped you feel confident in your abilities? Do you feel worthy of love? Do you feel like you are heard, seen, and appreciated?"

"Most of the time," nodded Ethan as he thought about Ambika's questions.

"We all feel down or uncertain sometimes, and that's ok," she continued. "The important thing is to acknowledge those feelings, work through them, and find ways to resolve challenges and not get stuck in them. These are the lessons of the third chakra."

Ethan was deep in thought as he listened. He still had his open palm flat against his solar plexus. After a few moments, he noticed his heartbeat under his palm - strong and rhythmic, and then his breathing as his belly and chest rose like a wave when he inhaled and exhaled. He looked up at Priya's mom again. She had noticed he was reflecting on something within himself and had patiently waited for Ethan to complete his thoughts.

"When we feel proud of ourselves and good in our skin, we hold our head, our chest, and shoulders straight. Try it and feel what it's like, Ethan. Stand up tall," said Priya's mom as she showed him the difference between someone being slumped over and someone standing straight and relaxed.

Ethan tried both ways of standing. First, he slumped his shoulders forward and bent his head down. It reminded him of someone feeling sad or shy. He thought about the times he allowed himself to fall into this posture; he was usually feeling down when he sat or stood like this. Next, he stood up tall, puffed his chest out slightly, held his head high, and took a deep breath. He instantly felt more alive and confident.

"Wow! Your posture really makes a difference in how you feel," said Ethan in wonder. "I never connected my feelings and body posture before."

"Yes, it can make a big difference. You can often tell how someone is feeling by looking at their posture. It's not only facial expression that tells us about a person's feelings, it's also in their tone of voice, the energy you sense around them, and how they hold their body."

"Think of an accomplishment you achieved and felt proud of. Remember a time when you did something that made your parents proud of you? You could feel their loving attention on you, which helped you feel worthy and special and appreciated. When someone feels good about themselves, their goals, or achievements, and knows their worth, they have good self-esteem, and it shows in how they hold their body."

"When our third chakra is balanced and feeling good, we can easily handle strong emotions. We don't block or hide our feelings. We feel and work through them. When our third chakra is strong, we are clear about our goals and have no problem accomplishing them."

Ethan slowly nodded his head as he imagined everything Priya's mom was telling him.

"If we feel jealous or shy or think that we are not as smart or fast or strong as another person, it doesn't feel good, does it, Ethan? Jealousy actually means that you feel very small inside. When someone feels small and insecure and hurt, they can become nasty and mean towards others."

"Tell me about it," piped up Ethan suddenly. "There were some kids at my old school who were like that. I used to think they were being mean because they enjoyed bullying others. I had no idea maybe they were feeling insecure or badly about themselves. Is it the same with mean adults?"

"That's a very astute observation Ethan," remarked Priya's mom. "You are right, even adults feel badly about themselves sometimes, and can be afraid or hurting when they are mean to others. They show everyone around them how small they feel inside when they try to make someone else feel badly."

"When we are ashamed about something we have done or said, our bodies feel unsettled too. That's what we call guilt—or feeling guilty. This is not a bad thing; guilt shows us that we did or said something that our Higher Self, our Spirit, doesn't agree with and doesn't feel good about. Your spirit knows that love is the essence of all things, and when we don't act in a loving way, we don't feel good about it. That bad feeling you have is your third chakra telling you that you need to act in a more loving way, and maybe, you need to apologize for something."

Some of the yoga students waved to Ambika as they got up to go home. Ethan turned the yellow leaf over in his hand again, thinking about the people in his life and how balanced their third chakras seemed to him.

Priya's mom picked up a yellow leaf that had fallen near her. "Our solar plexus chakra is where we learn to have a healthy sense of self and to believe in ourselves. We know our worth. We know we are enough as we are and deeply loved. We feel heard, seen, and appreciated. We are happy with ourselves. This is where your identity—your YOU—is strongly felt."

Do YOU like who you are, Ethan?" she asked him.

"Most of the time I do, but when I feel shy or nervous, I slump forward at my desk or try to hide in the back row in school so people can't see me," Ethan explained.

"Changing your body's posture can change how you feel. The next time you feel shy, think about how a warrior feels and how they walk; strong, tall, confident, and grounded. Copy that body posture and start walking like that. Pretty soon, you'll begin to feel more confident too," smiled Priya's mom.

Solar Plexus Chakra Discussion Questions

1. How do you feel when you look into the mirror? Do you like yourself?

2. What makes you feel proud of yourself?

3. How does the sun make you feel? Do you enjoy feeling the warm sunlight on your skin?

4. Have you ever felt guilty or ashamed about something? What did you do to change your feelings?

5. Why is it a good idea to love yourself? How can we do that?

6. Do you feel courageous even when in a scary or new situation you've never encountered before?

7. Do you know that you are in charge? That you choose how you feel? Do you know that you have the power to choose what kind of life you want to create and enjoy?

8. What goals do you have? What kinds of things do you want to experience when you grow up?

9. Have you ever been in a situation where you felt that you didn't have the power to make your own choice, or felt powerless in a situation that didn't feel good? What happened?

10. If your parents had to describe you to a friend, what do you think they would say about you—about the kind of person you are?

11. How do you "digest" strong emotions? How do you handle it when you feel really scared, angry, or upset? What do you do to feel better?

12. What do you think it means to be a hero? In what ways are you a hero? What would that feel like? Be the hero of your own life!

13. How does a confident person walk and stand? Do it. Imagine yourself walking like a confident warrior or hero with their shoulders back and chest out. Experiment with different postures to see how each one makes you feel.

14. Ask your parents these same questions.

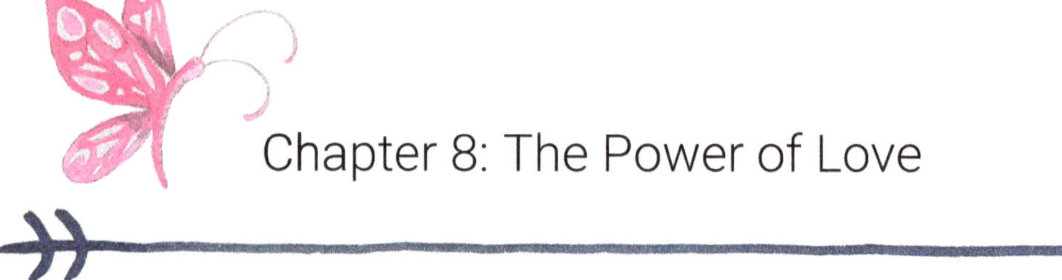

Chapter 8: The Power of Love

Ethan missed his parents.

That night, his mom called, and they spoke for a long time. He told her about what was happening at home, at school, and in the yoga class. Ethan's mom listened. Before they hung up, she told him how special he was to her, how much she loved him, and how much she was looking forward to seeing him again. She couldn't wait to give him a great big hug. It was wonderful to hear her voice. Ethan loved his mom. He thought she was the most beautiful, wonderful mom in the whole world. He began to feel better again.

After the call, though, it was just Ethan and Grandma Suzan. Normally, he was really happy visiting with Grandma Suzan, but for some reason, he was having trouble staying in the present. His thoughts kept going back to his memories of his old school and friends, and he began to feel lonely again.

Grandma could see that Ethan was missing his parents and friends, so she decided to help cheer him up. She got out two packs of cards and taught him how to play a game called Canasta. It was really fun and brought him right back to the present moment and out of the past. That was because he really had to focus to learn the new game and beat grandma! After the game, grandma asked Ethan how he was feeling.

"Much better," he replied.

"Do you know why?" Grandma Suzan asked with a smile as the two got up and moved into the kitchen to prepare dinner.

"Is it because I distracted myself and started thinking about the card game instead of my old friends who are far away?"

"Exactly!" smiled Grandma Suzan.

"When we feel down, it's usually because we are thinking about things that are in the past that don't feel good and we wished had happened differently, or we worry about things in the future that haven't happened and may never happen."

"It's good to remember happy times, but it's important to keep enjoying the journey you are on right now. While it's smart to plan for your future, you should be flexible and allow all kinds of wonderful surprises and experiences to come to you by being open to them. Sometimes, the best things in life are those that you weren't planning for."

"Be glad that you had those happy experiences with your friends, and understand that you will have many more happy experiences. In the meantime, focus on what you can do that makes you feel good right now. The most important thing is to feel good. When you notice you don't, do something to change your mood."

"Grandma, what do you do when you feel sad?" asked Ethan as he looked up at her while peeling carrots.

"Different things work for different people. We each have to figure out for ourselves what works best. When I feel a little down, I go out into my garden and admire all the beautiful flowers and plants, or I'll go for a long walk in the forest. Sometimes, I'll play music, have a bath, meditate, or make art. Other times, I'll make a mental list of all the things that I find beautiful, delightful, and uplifting and imagine how good each one of those things feels while thinking about it. I often play a game with myself where I look for at least 30 things to appreciate each day. This reminds me to focus my thoughts on all the good in my life. Playing with my wonderful grandsons always lifts my spirits and makes me feel happy too," replied grandma with a smile as she chopped the rest of the vegetables.

Ethan and Grandma Suzan made a delicious dinner together. Afterward, grandma asked Ethan if he wanted to help her make dessert. He suddenly got excited and jumped up and said, "yes!" Only this was not for him; it was for his parents. He wanted to learn how to make one of their favourite desserts—apple pie—so he could surprise them and let them know how much he loved them. He knew his mom and dad were missing him and his brothers too, so he decided to learn to do something that would make them feel special.

Grandma thought that was a wonderful idea and spent the next hour showing him how to read the recipe, measure out the ingredients, and mix it all together, and then, she helped him heat the stove and bake the apple pie. It smelled delicious!

Ethan felt really proud of himself for learning how to bake an apple pie. He noticed that he felt excited about it not because he got to eat it, but because he was making it as a gift for someone else, and that made him feel even better, knowing what a happy surprise it would be for his parents.

Ethan's brothers, Lukas and Hudson were impressed with his apple pie too and looked forward to eating a big slice.

After dinner, Lukas and Hudson decided to play a game together, leaving Grandma Suzan and Ethan alone. They sat at the kitchen table and played Canasta while talking about all kinds of things. Ethan spoke about the girl at school and how she had "stolen" his idea. In reality, she did not steal his idea; she just had the same one, and he realized that his idea was still great even if his classmate had the same one.

He and grandma talked all evening while playing cards. She told him fascinating stories from when she was younger and living on a farm in her village in Hungary.

She told him about how refreshing the well water

was, how good it felt to walk on the grass and earth barefoot, and how satisfying it felt to run in the fields, climb trees, and smell the flower-scented breeze blowing on a warm summer day. She told him about what her mom and dad were like, and even her grandparents.

Ethan listened wide-eyed. He loved hearing about his ancestors, about what life was like long before he was born, and how people lived. He was surprised to hear that they had very similar challenges and conflicts at school, with neighbours, and family and enjoyed many of the same things that he did. It seems everyone in the family enjoys apple pie. Grandma Suzan told Ethan it was his great-grandfather's favourite too, and that he looked very much like Ethan.

By the end of the night, Ethan's heart didn't feel quite so heavy anymore. He felt very close to Grandma Suzan and was happy he got to spend more time with her. She had quite a funny sense of humour too. She told him all about a crazy horse they used to have on the farm and about his grand-father, who loved to build things with his hands and go fishing. Grandma Suzan loved him very much, and while she was happy to be visiting Ethan and his brothers, she was looking forward to seeing grandpa again soon. He was back on the farm, keeping things going while she was away.

It was getting late. She gave him a big hug and sent him off to bed.

As he was getting ready to sleep, Ethan thought more about what Priya's mother had said about the chakras. He wondered if he would see his monkey guide in a dream again.

As it turned out, Ethan was in luck. That night, he dreamed again. This time, however, the dream was all about the fourth chakra.

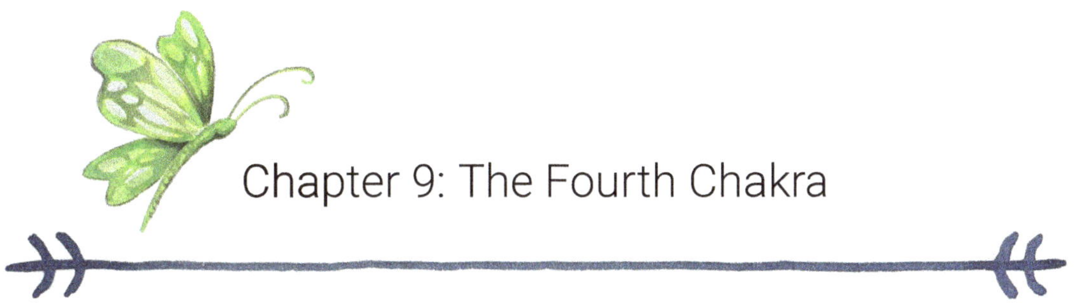

Chapter 9: The Fourth Chakra

The monkey guide appeared in the dream wearing a green suit stitched with banana leaves. He was playing the flute, and there were people dancing to the tune. The song was called:

"One of the most beautiful things about being human is having a heart."

Ethan couldn't remember the words exactly, but it went something like this:
We all have a physical heart in our bodies.
It beats a steady rhythm we hear and feel.
Our hearts feel the truth. It can understand things the mind does not.
The heart creates a powerful magnetic charge radiating out into the universe.
The heart is a place where we feel emotions such as love, awe, or joy.
People have complicated feelings that we can't always express with words.

The fourth chakra is also known as the 'Heart chakra'. Its colour is a beautiful green. When your heart chakra is balanced and feeling good, you enjoy connecting with others, accept others as they are, easily share love, and feel compassion and appreciation.

The monkey guide took Ethan by the hand, and he showed him many things in the dream.

Everyone feels glad and happy sometimes, and everyone feels sad or down sometimes. We can all feel different kinds of emotions. Think about how it feels when you laugh or cry, or sing, or play, or how it feels when you win or lose, or when you are with friends, or alone or afraid.

This is all an important part of being alive as a real person in real life. Feelings are important, and they are the doorway of the fourth chakra.

If we didn't feel emotions, life would be empty and boring. We would never want to do or learn anything. Animals and plants have feelings, too. They can feel hurt or excited, just like you.

The monkey guide showed Ethan how all kinds of living things have feelings of their own. He pointed to Ethan's own heart.

The fourth chakra is about our connection to others. It's about sharing a bond that shows we care about each other's happiness and well-being. At the level of the fourth chakra, you begin to think about other people and not only your own happiness. You realize how good it feels to empower someone, do something kind for another person, or simply enjoy connecting with others in meaningful ways.

At the level of the fourth chakra, you notice how others are feeling, and you begin to think about what you can do to help them feel better if they are sad. You care about them.

Remember, we like to connect with others, but the reason we like to do that is different at each chakra level. At the first three chakra levels, we connect to feel safe, to have our basic needs met, and to get to know who we are and feel confident enough to be ourselves in the world. At the fourth chakra level, we connect with people not for what they can give us or do for us, but simply because it feels good to share love and bond with that person. You enjoy hanging out with that person and sharing time, ideas, and energy together.

"Sometimes, our feelings make us act crazier than monkeys, though," laughed the monkey guide.

"That is why we have to learn about the heart chakra. When we understand what feelings are for, then we can work with them in the right ways. Feelings should never be ignored or bottled up, but we don't have to act mean or react badly just because of those feelings. How you act and feel is a choice. You are the one in control, and it is your decision how you want to feel, what you want to spend time thinking about, what kind of a life you want to create, and whom you want to invite into your world to create that life with."

Whenever someone is mean to you, think about your heart. Always know that your heart is strong enough and wise enough not to get involved in nastiness. You can create boundaries to keep yourself safe while still sending out love and peace to those around you.

That means the person also has a heart, and maybe their heart feels sore and hurt inside. Maybe that's why they act up. When someone is mean or nasty to other people, it's because they feel hurt inside. They feel unloved and disconnected from their source, and they feel lonely and unworthy in some way. They have forgotten how amazing and loved they are.

Remember that this person's behaviour isn't about you. It's not a reflection of your worth, so don't take that in, don't let what they say or do bring you down and feel bad. Understand that it has nothing to do with you. Their behaviour is showing people around them that they don't feel good about themselves.

When you know that someone who is mean feels alone, hurt, or frustrated, what do you think that person needs most? Is it love, or is it harsh, mean words? They need love. Don't feed that negative energy by reacting badly. Rather, stay kind and open in your heart. Send them love and soothing energy.

If necessary, it's ok to walk away to remove yourself from an unhappy or scary situation. You should always protect your peace and safety, but keep your heart open and feel good.

It is important that you take good care of your heart; feed it with love, kindness, and appreciation. Thank your heart for taking good care of you and for keeping you on the right path using the guidance of your feelings. Trust your feelings. Trust your heart.

The monkey guide then told Ethan about a powerful, secret way to connect to your heart and hear what it wants to share with you.

"Ethan," began the monkey guide, "imagine your heart in front of you, smile at each other, breathe together. What would you like to say to your heart? Tell it everything, don't hold back. You can also ask your heart questions. What do you think your heart would say to you?

Tell your heart how much you love it, which is the same as saying how much you love yourself. Your heart loves you very much too. Give each other a big heart hug, send love to each other, and thank each other for taking good care of one another."

The monkey guide told Ethan that while this may seem silly at first, it's actually a powerful technique used by many to help them remember to love themselves and others and to follow their inner guidance.

Heart Chakra Discussion Questions

1. Do you enjoy doing things that make others feel happy and connected with you?

2. Name some of the people that you love.

3. Name the people that love you.

4. Do you have any pets? How do you feel about them? Do you think they love you too? How do you know?

5. Do you think animals have feelings? How can you tell?

6. Do you think plants have feelings? How do you know?

7. How can you show Mother Nature that you love and appreciate her?

8. How can you show your family that you love them?

9. How do your parents show you that they love you?

10. How would you like your parents to show you they love you? (Spending time with you, telling you how important you are to them, listening to you, or something else?)

11. What do you think compassion is?

12. Why do you think people sometimes act mean or unkind?

13. Has anyone said or done something mean to you that felt bad? Why do you think they acted like that? What did you do in that situation? Is there anything you wished you had done differently? Did you send love and forgiveness to that person? If not, do you want to send love to them now?

14. What does forgiving someone mean? How do you forgive someone who was mean to you? Do you want to forgive them? Why/why not? Is it worth carrying hurt feelings with you or would you rather forgive and let go of those heavy, unpleasant feelings?

15. How do your parents handle it when someone is mean, thoughtless, or acts rudely? Is this a good strategy or do you think they can try something different next time?

16. Ask your parents these same questions.

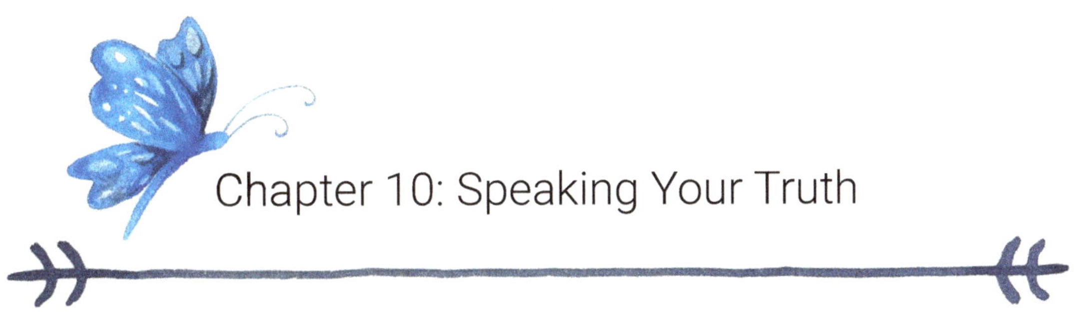

Chapter 10: Speaking Your Truth

The weekend came to an end, as all weekends do, and the sun finally came out from behind the clouds.

Ethan was going back to school, and this was the day he would stand up in front of the class and give his speech.

He was really nervous.

Grandma Suzan reminded him to stand up straight and to speak clearly. She printed out pictures of his two best friends from his old school. Ethan made some notes on a piece of paper, but his palms were so sweaty that he ruined them and had to start again!

Finally, the big moment came, and it was his turn to speak.

He stood up straight, remembering that it helped his third chakra to feel balanced by signalling his intent to be confident. Somehow, he got over his nerves and started talking about the countries he had been to and lived in.

About halfway through, he got stuck and forgot what he wanted to say. Ethan felt himself starting to get fidgety and turn red in the face, but then, he remembered the lessons of the chakras; he took a deep breath and straightened his shoulders while standing up even taller. That helped.

He also remembered his monkey guide, and that helped him relax even more as he finished his speech.

The teacher asked him many questions about Africa, China, and Hungary. He told the class about how he had seen lions and elephants and how his father had almost been bitten by a mamba—a dangerous snake.

"Are you happy that you moved here?" asked the teacher.

"Yes," said Ethan, "Even though I miss my friends, I know that I will make new friends soon." He looked over towards the desk to where Priya was sitting, and the two of them smiled at each other.

When he was finished, everyone clapped their hands and cheered! His speech was a big success. Even the girl who spoke before came up to Ethan and told him that she enjoyed his stories.

Ethan couldn't believe he had been so worried before. Now, he was happy that it was all over and proud of himself for facing his fears, standing up straight to strengthen his confidence and keeping his heart chakra open to bond with his classmates more easily.

He was feeling more relaxed and comfortable saying "hi" to them in the hallways and outside when he saw them. They also seemed to connect and bond with him, too, as they began inviting him to play.

Chapter 11: The Fifth Chakra

Can you guess where in your body the fifth chakra is found?

As we go up the spine, up past the heart, we reach the place where the neck begins. Inside your neck, you have vocal cords. That is where your voice comes from when you move air through them. The neck is also the part of your body that enables you to turn your head so you can see in many directions. That's a useful trick.

The fifth chakra has to do with communication. Its colour is a beautiful, vibrant blue. When your throat chakra is balanced and feeling good, you can easily communicate without overtalking or speaking too loudly; you are good at listening, and you are not afraid to say exactly what you think. You can also listen to others without getting offended or feeling self-conscious.

Speaking is a form of communication, and so is singing, using sign language, showing your facial expressions, and moving your body in a certain way. The energy that your thoughts and feelings emit also communicate a lot of information. Isn't it amazing that people are able to have conversations and communicate in so many ways with each other? We can talk about all kinds of things; we can express and communicate our ideas, thoughts, and feelings to one another, and share important information.

Being able to speak up is a useful and necessary part of life. Knowing when to be quiet and listen is very important too.

Animals, plants, and all of Mother Nature have their own language. They communicate and share their feelings and important information with each other. Even people can understand their language if they know how to tune in to their energy and "feel" the essence of their thoughts and feelings and know how to decipher their body language.

Think of all the incredible things you can do with your voice. You can teach someone a new skill. You can call friends to say "hello" and warn people about danger.

You can create healthy boundaries by learning how to say "no" when something isn't right for you. When something isn't right, your intuition or gut instinct lets you know through your feelings. You can then use your voice to speak your truth and give your honest opinion or ask for help if you need it.

When our fifth chakra is balanced, we speak the truth. Our voices are clear and true. Some people have beautiful singing voices. Some people speak really well. Others are quiet and like to listen more. When your heart chakra is open and your throat chakra balanced, you can be emotionally open, connected to others, and really hear their truth by listening to their words and feeling the energy behind them.

Everyone has a certain energy or "feeling" to them. It's like an energetic fingerprint. No two people's energies are alike. Some people are sensitive enough to pick up on another's energy. Others can learn to pick up on that by listening to their gut instinct and expanding their subtler senses.

You can tell if someone is feeling bad even if they smile and say they are ok by the energy you feel around them. Have you ever seen someone say they were happy but seemed to feel sad or angry instead? If the words and feelings don't match, listen to the feelings; they will tell you the truth. Pay attention to the energy behind the words and actions of people. It will help you understand them and their motivations better. When we are struggling with the fifth chakra, we find it difficult to express what we truly want to say. We may feel shy or silly, and we may be afraid to speak up and tell others what we really think or want.

People who tell lies have trouble with their throat chakra. So do those who bottle up their feelings and don't have the courage to honestly say what they want. These situations can imbalance the throat chakra.

How can you tell if your throat chakra is imbalanced? If you have to clear your throat often, have a recurring cough, feel that no one listens to you, or that your voice and needs aren't being heard, these signs tell us we need to give our throat chakra extra love and care."

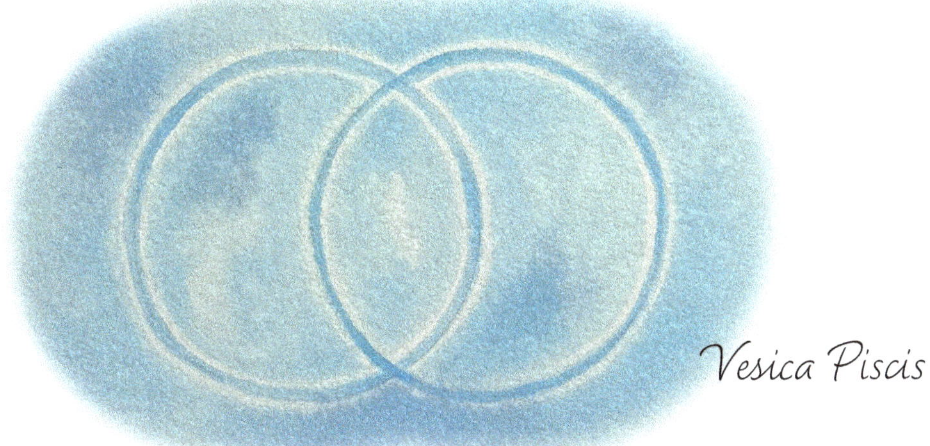

Throat Chakra Discussion Questions

1. Do you talk a lot?

2. What would it feel like if you couldn't talk for a whole day? Not even a single word? How would you communicate?

3. Do you listen to others with your ears and your heart? What is the difference?

4. Do you like to sing, or hear others singing? When you like someone's voice, what does it sound like to you? Why do you think you like it? Do you feel something when you hear their voice? What does it feel like when you listen to a voice you like?

5. What does it mean to be truthful and honest?

6. Have you ever told a lie? What happened? How did you feel about it? If you could go back in time, what would you do differently?

7. Can lying hurt other people?

8. How can lying hurt you?

9. Would you want people to lie to you? Why not?

10. Are there situations where not telling the truth is acceptable? Ask your parents what they think about this.

11. What is the difference between lying and withholding the truth or not speaking up to clarify a misunderstanding?

12. When should we be quiet instead of talking?

13. Have you ever felt nervous to tell someone how you really felt about something? Why were you nervous?

14. Have you ever felt nervous to tell someone about something you wanted? Why were you nervous?

15. Are you afraid to say "no" to people when they ask you for something?

16. Have you ever felt that it wasn't safe, to be honest? Why?

17. Ask your parents if they've ever felt nervous or unsafe to speak up and tell the truth about something. What did they do? Why were they nervous?

18. Have you ever felt strong emotion but instead of letting it out with a good cry or scream, you instead swallowed it down to keep from crying? If yes, why did you do this instead of letting it out? Do you think others cover up their true emotions too, sometimes? Why do you think people do this?

19. Have you ever felt like you had a lump in your throat and your throat chakra energy got stuck? Why do you think this happens? Ask your parents if they've ever experienced having a lump in their throats. What caused this?

20. Ask your parents these same questions.

Chapter 12: In The Mind's Eye

After school, Ethan went over to Priya's house again. The two of them were becoming good friends, and another boy from class, Evan, wanted to join them. The three friends walked together to Priya's bright green house.

Priya's mother, Ambika, was leading a meditation class.

Priya told Ethan and Evan to be very quiet. When people meditate, it is important to respect their space and not make noise.

Neither Ethan nor Evan had ever heard of meditation before. Priya said that people meditate to stay calm and balance their minds by staying focused on the present moment, but she didn't think she was very good at meditation.

"I can't sit still for two minutes!" She said softly as they walked past the studio. Ethan peeped in through the door.

Two students were sitting with legs crossed and perfectly straight backs, with eyes closed. They held their hands in an interesting way—with the thumbs and forefingers touching. They sat quietly and peacefully for such a long time, that they looked like statues.

Ethan wanted to try it, so he quietly sat down at the back of the room and closed his eyes. Priya's mom said something about focusing on his breath while inhaling and exhaling. He tried sitting quietly like that, but after three minutes, he got bored. He noticed that the more he tried to sit still and focus on his breathing like everyone else in the class, the more he fidgeted and had all kinds of thoughts pop up. His mind was jumping all over the place! Instead of being relaxed and quiet, he became restless.

After the class, Priya's mom told him that despite being fidgety and thinking many thoughts, he did a good job in his first class. She said that many people think meditation is about sitting quietly, but you can meditate when fishing, gardening, doing the dishes, or other activities as long as your breathing is slow and rhythmic and your mind is focused on the moment, and not lost in the past or future. She said there were many ways to meditate and that she would tell him more about it the next time he came to the class.

Ethan was still curious about chakras and wanted to know about them, so he asked Priya's mom to tell him more.

Chapter 13: The Sixth Chakra

Our journey continues up towards the top of the spine and the head.

In the middle of your head, in the space between your eyes is where the sixth chakra is. The colour of this chakra is indigo, which is a very dark and rich shade of blue.

The sixth chakra is also known as the 'Third Eye chakra' and is connected to the pineal gland—known as the master gland. It is the seat of wisdom, clear seeing, and understanding things deeply and profoundly. A balanced sixth chakra allows you to sense things that you don't normally see with your eyes or hear with your ears. It is the space through which answers to life questions come to you in the form of dreams, visions, and strong intuitive knowing.

When your sixth chakra is balanced and open, you see things for what they are, without judgment of good or bad. You don't blame or point the finger at someone and say, "It was your fault." Instead, you go deep to understand the reason for their actions and behaviour. You don't label people as good or bad; you try to understand what caused them to act the way they did. Your ethics and sense of justice are also connected to your third eye chakra.

An open third eye chakra engages the entire brain (both the left and right hemispheres) to work harmoniously together, enabling you to reach your highest potential using more than just your physical senses.

How amazing that we can think, be aware, and be conscious! What would life be like if we didn't know what thinking was? Can you even imagine something like that?

Where do you think all this "thinking" happens? Is it in the brain in your head? Or is the brain a filter that sorts through and translates all the information coming in from your senses? Do we even need a brain? What do you think?

Did you know that there are people born without brains? Yes, it's true. Well then, where do they do all their thinking? Maybe our thoughts—our awareness—are separate from our brains and physical bodies even though they can work together. How are they linked; what do you think? How can your thoughts affect your brain and body?

When our sixth chakra is open and in harmony, then our heads are clear. We can think easily, and our minds don't get stuck in all kinds of nonsense, like thinking about the same old imaginary problem all the time.

We can figure things out for ourselves without making the same mistakes over and over again. But if you do make a mistake, that's ok too because you learn from it.

Did you know that your brain has two main parts called the left and right hemispheres? It looks a little like the inside of a walnut. Each brain part is mainly responsible for controlling the actions of the opposite side of the body; though the brain is highly versatile and can learn all kinds of new things.

Sometimes, these two brain hemispheres are not in harmony with each other. The good news is that there are many things you can do to balance your brain and encourage it to work more efficiently. Some examples are brain gym and a wonderful exercise called alternate nostril breathing.

You alternate covering your right nostril with the thumb of your right hand, and the left nostril with the last two fingers of the same hand.

1. Inhale slowly for a count of four through the left nostril while covering your right nostril.
2. Retain your breath for a count of sixteen.
3. Exhale slowly for a count of eight through the right nostril while covering the left nostril.
4. Inhale slowly for a count of four through the right nostril.
5. Retain the breath for a count of sixteen.
6. Exhale slowly for a count of eight through the left nostril.

That is one round. That's it! See how easy it is? Now, you try.
Do up to 10 rounds.

At the level of the sixth chakra, you can begin to access your "superhero" abilities. You are mindful and creative, easily come up with brilliant, original ideas, and have expansive thinking that is holistic, connecting information seamlessly rather than only seeing the individual parts. To do all that, keep in mind that your other chakras need to be aligned too, with your heart open and your spirit relaxed.

Third Eye Chakra Discussion Questions

1. Which is your favourite sense: seeing, hearing, smelling, tasting, touching, feeling, or intuiting/sensing? (There are actually more but let's start with these ones.) Can you choose a favourite? If yes, why is this your favourite?

2. Can you imagine not having one or more of these senses to help guide you? What do you think that would be like?

3. Do you have visions or dreams that come true or help you figure out how to solve problems? Do your parents or friends have dreams and visions?

4. What kinds of things do you think about most often? How do those thoughts feel?

5. Do you ever see geometric patterns when you close your eyes or before falling asleep?

6. Do you ever notice number patterns such as 222 or 12:12 throughout your day? What do you think it means for you?

7. Do you ever just "know" that something is about to happen?

8. Have you ever experienced a sense of déjà vu? (It feels like the thing that just happened already happened before; it feels really familiar, and you may think that you might have dreamed it or imagined it earlier.)

9. Have you ever experienced telepathy or "heard" in your mind what seemed like someone's thoughts or feelings? Have your parents?

10. Do you ever have headaches? If yes, when and why do they seem to happen? Do you notice a pattern with physical symptoms?

11. Do you ever have bad dreams? If yes, what are they about? Do you think there is a message in them for you? How can you overcome bad dreams?

12. Do you fly in your dreams? If yes, how do you do it?

13. Do you notice what colours you see in your dreams? Some people say that the colours in your dreams tell you which chakras need more focus.

14. Can you control your dreams and change what happens in them? This is called lucid dreaming. How can you learn to do this? Do you know of anyone who can do this?

15. Do you dream from the first-person perspective, second, third, or change from one to the other?

16. Do you overthink things and get stuck thinking about them over and over again? If yes, why do you do this?

17. Ask your parents and friends about the types of dreams they have.

18. Ask your parents these same questions.

Inhale Deeply
Exhale Slowly
Smile Brightly

Inhale Deeply
Sigh Happily As You Exhale
Smile Softly

Inhale Even Deeper
Sigh Happily As You Exhale
Close Your Eyes
and Shine Brightly

Chapter 14: The End of the Week

The next few days went by quickly.
Ethan was making new friends, and he
was able to go outside in the sunshine
and play in the park as often as he liked, so
long as his chores and homework were done.

Grandma Suzan and Ethan decided to cook a
special dinner on Friday along with a big apple pie because
that was the day when Ethan's mom and dad were finally
coming home.

Priya and Ethan were now visiting each other all the time,
and sometimes, they would both join the yoga and meditation classes.

One day, Priya's mom showed Ethan a most interesting picture
from an old book she had. It was a picture of Hanuman, the Hindu
monkey god. It reminded Ethan of his dream guide, and that very evening,
he dreamed of the chakras again. It was about time too! So far, Ethan
knew about the first six, but there was one more to go.

That night in his dream, the monkey guide showed Ethan all seven spinning wheels: Red, orange, yellow, green, blue, indigo, and the one at the top was bright white with a little violet.

He showed Ethan how all things in the universe find their proper place and how each being follows his or her own true path.

Seed of Life

Chapter 15: The Seventh Chakra

The seventh chakra connects us to everything. It reminds us that we are all one big family, deeply connected, and what one feels or experiences sends ripples through to all others that are connected. If you are feeling good, you cause others around you to begin to elevate their feelings too.

It is like the king of the chakras, and that's why it is also called the "Crown chakra." For full alignment, all the chakras must work together in harmony as if they were dancing together to the same tune.

The crown chakra connects us with something that is bigger than our own life. When we feel open and connected to the divine both inside and around us, we know our seventh chakra is working well. It is the space where we can lose our sense of time. We feel timeless and weightless. We can simply "be" without perceived restrictions or limits. It is the space where you trust and know that all is well and working out perfectly; no matter how it may appear in the moment, you simply KNOW that everything is working out.

When your crown chakra feels good, you know your wisdom; you know you are a divine soul; you know you are unlimited and free yet deeply connected, and all the while, you feel completely grounded and safe. You feel in control of your life, your soul, and your destiny. You know who you are, and you feel right about it. You are confident and kind and know how to be open and look at the world with awe and wonder. You are peaceful and cheerful.

When you are completely in the present moment, you forget time. You fully immerse yourself in your activity while everything else dissolves into the background. This is sometimes called a classic "Zen moment." Being so fully in the present moment that you forget everything happening around you because you have shifted your consciousness. Your focus—your awareness—is sharp and turned inward.

The inner world is a rich and wondrous place filled with universal truths. You feel the oneness of all things and complete peace and harmony with everything and everyone around you.

People who become wonderful helpers to humankind, like the saints, the great teachers, and the holy men and women; all these people had very powerful and bright seventh chakras. That's why you sometimes find pictures of them with a halo of light around their heads. Their seventh chakra is shining brightly!

If you see someone who is always smiling, gentle and kind, who's peaceful, and who seems to have a bright light behind their eyes, and can understand everyone, then you know their seventh chakra is active and balanced.

The crown chakra doesn't really have a colour of its own. Instead, you could say that it combines all the other colours into one. For some, it feels white; for others, violet. Your seventh chakra is working well when you feel a deep sense of compassion and connection with everything and everyone and you can easily access your inner wisdom. For most people, it takes a very long time to open and develop their seventh chakra. Sometimes, a whole lifetime, or two, or three!

When the seventh chakra is blocked, it can cause a person to be sensitive to light and sound and be stubborn and skeptical. They may feel a lack of life purpose and disconnection from their divine Selves.

Crown Chakra Discussion Questions

1. How do you feel when you look up at the stars?

2. Are you able to observe a strong emotional exchange between people yet remain unattached and not pulled into the drama and intense feelings? How can we do this?

3. Have you ever felt blissful, in rapture, such peace and joy at once that you felt removed from your body and in a different world?

4. Have you ever seen a person's energy field, also called an aura (it's like a soft light around them and can be made up of different colours)?

5. Have you ever felt a deep peace and knowing even when everything around seemed chaotic?

6. Is there anything that makes your eyes light up in wonder? What makes you feel awe?

7. Do you ever feel stubborn about certain things? That you have to have your own way no matter what? Why do you feel this way? What do you think would happen if you let someone else have their way sometimes?

8. Do you know you are a divine soul here with a purpose and to do great things in life? You are, and you will!

9. Why do you think you chose to be born? Do you think it was an accident or did your spirit want to come here?

10. Do you know where your soul came from?

11. Do you think you chose your parents to be your parents? If yes, why did you choose them? Why do you think they chose you to be their child?

12. Ask your parents about their feelings when they first started thinking about you and looking forward to your arrival. How excited were they? What was that experience like for them? How did it feel when they held you as a newborn for the very first time? What was it like for them to look deeply into your newborn eyes when you first opened them?

13. Ask your parents these same questions.

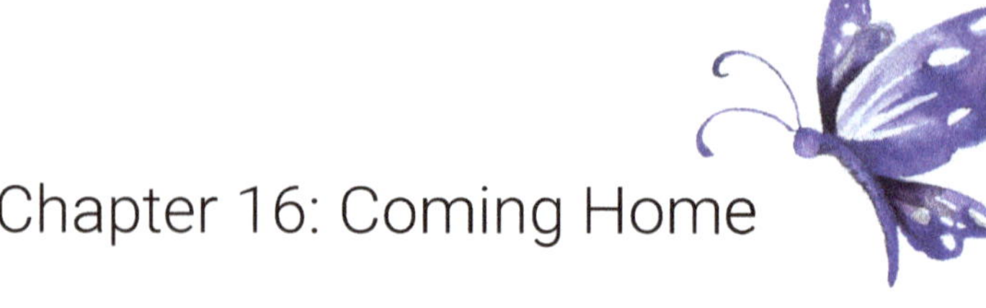

Chapter 16: Coming Home

When Friday finally arrived, Ethan, Lukas, Hudson, and Grandma Suzan went to the airport to pick up Mom and Dad. The two of them were overjoyed to be home, and they brought all kinds of things back with them. The most important gift, however, was that they were together again and could give and receive hugs and radiant smiles, and share lots of stories and laughs.

Ethan felt so happy! All his chakras must have been lit up like bright shining stars! His parents were home, and his heart felt full of love.

He told his parents all about what had happened at school and about his new friend, Priya, and he told them about the chakras too. His parents told them all about the places they visited, the people they met, and the everyday things that happened throughout their trip.

The whole family stayed up late because there was so much to say and share!

Ethan felt much more confident and self-assured, ready to share what was in his heart.

Every now and then, the monkey guide made an appearance in his dreams to help guide him when he had questions. It felt good to know he could tap into his higher self for clarity and use the power of his emotions to know what felt right and what didn't. It also felt good knowing he had a loving family, friends he could explore the world with, and peace in his heart.

That night, he slept deeply, dreaming of the stars and the moon and all the amazing things he was going to do in this lifetime. He told the stars in his dream all his plans for the future. He told the moon about all the people he was going to meet, love, and enjoy life with.

He then flew over to the sun and told him about the many gifts he had to share with the world, uplift it, inspire others with it, and bring joy to those around him and himself in the process. Ethan remembered his aunt Yvette often told him that the most important thing was to feel good. If you can get to a good-feeling place, then you can achieve anything and have the full support of the universe to back you up.

Ethan was very excited to remember all the reasons he decided to be born and couldn't wait to grow up and start doing all those things. Just as he was thinking this, he felt something begin to gently pull him back down to the earth, away from his star, moon, and sun friends. He felt soothing, warmth all over his body, and deep sleepiness came over him.

The next thing he knew; it was early morning the next day. Ethan was lying in his bed and feeling really good. He thought he remembered telling the stars something about his future life, but he couldn't quite remember the dream. "Hmmm … was it a dream?" he wondered.

Suddenly, the smell of palachinta wafted into the air and found his nose. Ethan heard his parents laughing and talking with Grandma Suzan as they made breakfast together. He heard his brothers opening their bedroom doors as he too, jumped out of bed to join his family with big hugs and smiles to enjoy their time together and leap into the day!

The End

⟫ ———————————————————— ⟪

What Do You Think About The First Book?

Friends, we have come to the end of Book 1.
How did you like it? What did you most enjoy about the story?

I'd love to hear about your favourite parts and welcome you to share them with me via email at: feedback@singingsoulbooks.com

As a gift to you, dear reader, here is a sneak peak of the first chapter of Book 2. Enjoy!

Loving appreciation to all that you are and bring to the world.
Keep shining your light!

Warmly,

Yvette

Book Two:

Safely Connected to Earth

Ethan and his Family Explore the Root Chakra

Chapter One: Grandma's Garden 

There was no place in the world quite like Grandma Suzan's herb and vegetable garden.

The whole family stayed on grandma and grandpa's farm, out in the countryside, every summer. Ethan and his younger brothers, Lukas and Hudson, always looked forward to it.

Each morning grandma would wake the kids bright and early. They would all go down to that magical herb garden while the dew was still wet on the grass. The garden was so green, so full of interesting growing things, and it smelled wonderful.

Grandma Suzan knew each plant by name. She would often talk to them as if they were her own children. Lukas wore his favourite blue wellington boots this summer, as he didn't like to get his feet muddy.

"Why do you talk to plants if they can't hear you?" he asked, giggling and holding grandma's hand.

"They love it!" replied grandma, "It makes them grow better, and they feel safe and loved."

"Do plants really feel things like happiness or fear?" asked Ethan.

"They certainly can," laughed grandma. "They're different from us, of course. I don't think they understand my exact words, but they can feel my energy, love, and care. They can tell when people are anxious, excited, or sad. Every living thing, even this little tomato bush feels all kinds of emotions. They can feel afraid, thirsty, hurt, content, excited, happy, loving, or peaceful."

"If you go near a plant thinking about hurting it, it will sense it before you get close and feel anxious and afraid of you. Likewise, if you send love and appreciation to that same plant, smile, and speak sweetly to it as you walk towards it, that plant will feel your adoration and welcome you with its love. When they feel loved by you, they do their best to grow healthy and strong, so they can share their love and care for you through the nourishment and bounty they grow for you."

"Did you know that the plants you plant and care for consider you their beloved family - even though you aren't a plant?" asked Grandma Suzan.

"Really?" replied Lukas with surprise.

"Really," continued Grandma Suzan, "in fact," she continued, "all plants have a special bond with the people who love them. They grow special enzymes, vitamins, minerals, and healing essences specifically for that person. By eating the bounty of that plant's offering, that plant is helping to heal you of any imbalance or disease in your body and mind. This is why it is vitally important to grow at least some of your own food. No other plant will be as healthy and perfect for you as the ones you grow yourself with great care and love."

"Grandma, how do plants know what kinds of vitamins and healing properties they need to grow for their human family?" wondered Ethan, fascinated.

"That's an excellent question, little man," laughed Grandma Suzan. "You will not believe how simple the answer is! Can you guess?"

Ethan and Lukas thought it was the special humus soil they mixed into the earth before planting a new little seedling.

"That's a good guess, boys, but it's even simpler than that," smiled Grandma Suzan.

"Have you noticed that your grandpa, Aunt Yvette, and I are always walking around barefoot when we are in the gardens? The sweat and oils from the bottom of our feet contain tiny messages about our bodies' health. This tells the plants what we need to be strong and healthy. Suppose the message from the sweat and oils tells the plants that something is out of harmony in us, that something is not balanced. In that case, they will instantly know what compounds, vitamins, minerals, and other healing essences they need to create to help us heal by eating the bounty they grow for us."

"Mother nature is incredibly wise and accurate and does not make mistakes. What these plants grow for us is maximally beneficial for those who spend time here, walking barefoot and caring for them. No two people are the same, and no two plants are the same. Isn't that incredible? So simple yet effective. Of course, you have to genuinely love and care for your plants. When they feel that you care about them, they care about you too."

"Does that mean that if we grow peppers, like those ones right there," said Ethan as he pointed to a part of the garden that had three rows of bright yellow pepper plants, "and your neighbours down the road grows the same kind of peppers, that what's inside them isn't the same - even if they look exactly alike?" asked Ethan.

"That's exactly right, Ethan," smiled grandma. "They may even taste the same or very similar, but our neighbours' peppers will not be as healing and nourishing for us as the peppers we grow ourselves. Those peppers were not cared for in the same way as those in our garden. They are different. By the same token, our neighbours' plants will be most delicious and healthy for them."

"Those pepper plants you pointed to are actually your Aunt Yvette's. It's her favourite kind. She prepared the seeds, planted them, and has been caring for them. That means that those peppers will be the best and most beneficial for her. Even if you and I eat them, and they taste good and are healthy for us as well, they will be best suited for your Aunt since they grew especially for her," explained grandma as she knelt down next to one of the yellow pepper plants to gently caress a leaf in appreciation.

"Do you see those rose bushes over there, boys?" asked grandma as she pointed to the Southern part of the garden.

"Yes, what about them?" asked Lukas.

"When your Aunt Yvette is getting ready to make rose syrup, rose tea, rose jam, rose water, and a nice rose scrub, she has a conversation with her rose bushes about two weeks earlier. She honours their sovereign spirit by first asking them permission to use their flowers to make these medicines and foods. If they agree, they both enter into a sacred relationship of working together harmoniously to increase the growth of the flowers. The first thing she does when she leaves her yurt in the morning is go straight to her rose bushes to thank them for sharing their beauty with her and everyone around us - that includes the people, the animals, and other plants. She gently caresses their leaves and praises them for growing so strong and healthy, for being so beautiful, and for sharing their love with us."

"Do you mean she has conversations with the rose bushes, grandma?" asked Lukas incredulously.

"Oh, you should hear her in the mornings! It's a constant chatter of love and admiration. You can tell from her tone of voice, movements, smile, and the energy she radiates that she really loves those rose bushes. You can also tell that they love your Aunt because they would do anything to make her happy, especially what she has so lovingly asked of them. It is a mutually joyful connection; and do you know what starts to happen within a few days?"

"What?" asked both boys, enthralled, their eyes big, walking towards the rose bushes with renewed awe.

"They begin to grow more flowers. A lot more. Ten times more! So much, in fact, that you can hardly see any of the green leaves. It is truly miraculous to witness a plant respond so powerfully to genuine love and appreciation. It looks like a flaming pink bush with so many flowers!"

"Your aunt then begins to gather the flowers in the early morning when the dew is still wet and the energy in the plants is high. Once she has enough flowers for all the foods and medicines she wants to make, she tells her rose bushes she has all she needs, thanks them, and they instantly stop producing extra flowers. Within a few days, they return to looking like their "normal" selves with beautiful flowers here and there but not ten times as much."

"Wow!" whispered Ethan in awe.

That sounded pretty magical to him. He knew that his grandparents and Aunt often spoke softly with their plants, the trees, the animals around them, and many other things, some of which he couldn't see, but he had no idea how powerful it could be to focus love and appreciation on something. It made him think about how he spoke with his dog, friends, pet fish, and the plants in his backyard.

Suddenly, it occurred to him that he even had conversations with himself, sometimes in his head and sometimes out loud. He realized that the way he spoke to himself at times wasn't very encouraging or nice.

"I should speak more lovingly with myself," he thought, the way grandma, grandpa, my parents, and Aunt Yvette speak to me and their plants.

Suddenly, Lukas piped up, "Grandma, is there anything else we can do to help our plants grow extra healthy for us?"

"Yes, there is, Lukas. In fact, I was going to show you boys how to plant seeds based on the idea that we are all one family here to love and support each other's growth."

Grandma Suzan carefully removed a small package from her apron pocket. It was meticulously wrapped in soft fabric. She unwrapped it and showed the contents to Ethan and Lukas. They both leaned in to get a closer look. In her hand, they saw dozens of small, reddish-brown seeds.

"Today is the right time to plant these seeds. We garden according to the lunar phases. There are other important astrological aspects to consider, too, as all the Heavenly bodies have unique energies that can affect your plant's growth and potential. But that's a much longer lesson for another day. Just know that it's important to align the energies of the universe when planning your planting season."

Grandma Suzan walked them to a new section of the garden. There, the boys saw that she had already made three rows of small holes in the soil. She also had three large pails of water that had been warmed by the sun's rays.

"First, I blew a steady stream of warm air onto the seeds to help bond us and familiarize these precious seeds with my energy and essence. Next, I held them up to the sunlight, letting the rays warm them and imbue them with celestial essence. In the evening, I held them up to the moon, letting her cooling rays nourish and prepare these little seeds, stirring infinite potential within them. After that, I added a small amount of my saliva onto them, so they could get all the important messages my spirit wanted the seeds to know about me. That way, they knew exactly what I need from them to keep me strong and healthy. Now the seeds know and understand me and are ready to share their love and medicine with me as long as I care for them too."

"Do you do this with all your seeds, grandma?" asked Lukas.

"Yes, sweetheart, I do this with all my seeds. So does your aunt and grandpa. We each have a section in the garden for those plants which are our favourite and that we grow especially for ourselves. We also have many plants that we share. However, the ones that grow specifically for you are the most potent, powerful, and healing."

"Think of this as a sacred ritual. Acting in this way helps to connect everything and everyone. It's a very special thing to do and is thoroughly grounding. Your friend Priya might say it is a beautiful Root Chakra way of growing food since this results in both food and a deep feeling of peace."

Grandma moved quickly to plant one seed in each hole, row by row. When she was done, she watered each spot.

"I drew this water up from the well yesterday. You need to let water sit for at least a day to clear it energetically and allow any sediment to fall to the bottom. It's also important to allow the water to absorb both sunlight and moonlight, as well as your loving intent."

"Water is a powerful transmitter of feelings, energies, and many other elements. We must treat it with respect and use it wisely. It can help cleanse us, stave our thirst, cool us off, and even heal us."

"When you bless your water and send it positive thoughts, it retains the energy of those thoughts and feelings and passes it on to what it touches next. Wouldn't you enjoy drinking water that has the energy of gratitude, kindness, and joy in it? It feels good to drink water that is uplifting, energizing, and loving. Your spirit and the cells of your body enjoy it more. You'll feel good too."

Grandma finished watering the newly planted radish seeds, then she said, "Another reason I wait for the sun to warm up the water before watering newly planted seeds is because cold water would shock them. It wouldn't be good for them, just as you wouldn't like it if I suddenly doused you with a bucket of ice-cold water."

Ethan and Lukas nodded in agreement. They were beginning to understand why their aunt insisted on them writing positive, happy words of encouragement and appreciation onto their water bottles. Although, they couldn't quite remember what she said was the reason they should chew their water and mix it with saliva before swallowing each mouthful.

"Plants have friends too," pointed out grandma. "They are aware of every other plant, fungi, mineral, insect, and animal around them - both on the ground and underneath in the soil. They work together to create a happy community and help each other when necessary."

Grandma's garden had all sorts of plants, flowers, and herbs. There were climbing tomato plants, creeping squash plants, dill, sage, rosemary, chives, peppermint, and many other kinds of vegetables and herbs. Sometimes the plants needed to be watered, and sometimes grandma would get the kids to shovel fresh manure into the soil to prepare it for the following spring. Now that was smelly work!

"That reminds me," said grandma as she stopped shovelling for a moment, "There is one more way to help plants get to know you so they can grow into powerful medicinal food for you. Can you guess what that is?" she asked mysteriously with a laugh.

After many guesses, neither of which hit the mark, she finally let them in on the secret. "It's manure."

"Manure?!" cried Ethan in utter amazement. "What do you mean?"

"Everything that leaves our body contains important information about our state of health. When we mix our manure into the earth and add a little to the garden, the plants will get a lot of information about you. They will know exactly what you need to feel great, and that's how they will grow."

Ethan couldn't get over what Grandma Suzan had just told him. He looked down at his shovel and realized the connection between himself, the composting toilet in the outhouse, the garden, the plants, and eventually, the food that made its way back to his body.

"Wow, I never thought about it like that!" he said thoughtfully,
"It's a full cycle."

"Exactly!" said grandma triumphantly with a happy smile. "Nature has many, many cycles. It's good to get to know as many of them as you can and work in unison with those natural cycles. It will make for a happy and joyful life."

Once the boys finished helping grandma in the garden, they went to explore a shady part of the farm to see what they could discover.

"Look, I found an earthworm!" cried Ethan, delighted, and held the wriggling worm up for his little brother to see.

"Eeew!" screeched Lukas. "Keep that away from me! I don't like slimy things!"

"I'm going to use this one as bait when we go fishing," exclaimed Ethan happily.

More than anything, Ethan was looking forward to fishing with grandpa. His Grandpa Otto would be arriving the next day, along with his youngest brother Hudson, who was three years younger than Lukas. All of them were going to hike down to the river.

But first, there was root work to do. It was time to plant the beans and onions.

To be continued...

Yvette Farkas

Yvette is the creator of Singing Soul Books and a magical story enchantress. She can often be found wandering the deepest sanctuaries of forests and mountains and enjoying the "thundering loud" quiet of sacred spaces both outside and within.

She enjoys sharing her love of the unusual and mystical such as bullwhip cracking, foraging for herbs while the dew is still fresh, harnessing the power of natural energies, telling captivating stories in her yurt, and sharing wisdom gleaned from 30+ years of training in the martial and healing arts.

Yvette is an explorer of consciousness, a writer, gardener, photographer, traveller, and a budding beekeeper. She is a child of the Universe, leaving seeds of joy and the sweet aroma of empowered belief in the people she meets while learning and growing.

Yvette is also a health-based, heart-centered coach and mentor, and a practitioner of ancient healing practices taking people back to their health and their hearts. She uses the power of stories to share love and wisdom and reveal the inherent interconnectedness of all things, inspiring and empowering others toward their highest potential. Her work is meant to shed light on that which people rarely see, to uplift their Spirits, forge deep heartfelt connections, and inspire their hearts.

You can reach Yvette here:

www.singingsoulbooks.com, www.yvettefarkas.com and www.bioresonancescans.com
LinkedIn: https://www.linkedin.com/in/yvettefarkas

Jana Rothwell

Jana is the illustrator of Singing Soul Books. She finds passion in using her endless imagination to teach and create art that captivates people of all ages. She strives to empower others to grow, to learn to love themselves unconditionally, to speak their truth and to follow their dreams. She enjoys exploring the beauty in nature and feels most at home near and in the water. Jana encompasses all the characteristics of a typical Pisces: she is creative, gentle, sensitive, kind, compassionate, intuitive, and wise. Infinite amounts of light and love radiate from her. She connects deeply with children and animals because of their innocence and pure hearts.

She has the unique ability of seeing the best and the potential in everyone she meets. As a strong believer in the vastness and power of the Universe, Jana embraces the idea that we are all connected. She is a free spirit, continually learning and growing, always ready to share her creative ideas and stories, and never afraid to laugh at her own silliness.

You can reach Jana here:

janarothwelldesigns.com

Email: info@janarothwell.com

Instagram: @janalee_111 and @marigold_creative_art

Wayne Bloemhof

Wayne is a piece of the infinite creative wonder that just is. He claims nothing special as his own, always amazed at the words that come out of his fingertips as he types. Where do they come from? We can only speculate.

He lives in a place called Knysna, which is a little piece of heaven. He feeds the Turacos and white-eyes, sharing his apples, oranges and bananas with the forest creatures.

He often just walks down to the river, for no reason in particular, and leads a quiet life of wonder. He writes, ghostwrites and creates to help people put words to the stories in their hearts.

You can reach Wayne here:

www.waynebloemhof.wordpress.com
Email: waynebloemhof@gmail.com

Resources

Glossary 90

Palachinta Recipe 92

The Mystic's Library of Excellence 94

    Mind and Practical Metaphysics........................... 94

    Consciousness, Quantum Physics, and Epigenetics..................... 97

    ESP, Remote Viewing, Quantum Physics, and
Consciousness Expansion...................................... 99

    Soul Matters, Past Lives, Dreams, Reincarnation, and
Near Death Experiences...................................... 101

    Parthenogenesis and the Divine Feminine................. 102

    The Alpha Male and Divine Masculine..................... 104

    Communication Styles of Men and Women................ 105

    Taoism and Inner Alchemy................................. 106

    Martial Arts Philosophy.................................... 108

    Shamanism and Psychedelic Plants....................... 110

    Health (Wholeness) and Healing.......................... 111

    Yoga Philosophy 117

    Ayurveda (The Science of Life)............................ 119

    Sacred Geometry and Physics............................. 120

    Finances and Weath 121

    Behaviour and Body Language............................. 123

    Transmitted and Channelled Information................. 123

    Conscious Leadership, Mentorship, and Coaching 125

    Other.. 126

    Devices for Health and Healing 128

Glossary for the first book:

Spiritual, metaphysical, and unusual terms and their meanings from the first book in the "Ethan and the Seven Chakras" book series.

1. **Alternate Nostril Breathing:** A breathing exercise that involves alternating the breathing between the left and right nostrils to balance the brain and improve mental clarity.
2. **Asana:** A term used to describe the practice of yoga postures. Asanas also mean "a pose you can comfortably hold for a long time."
3. **Awakening:** Process of becoming aware of spiritual and metaphysical concepts and the potential within oneself.
4. **Cabin Fever:** A feeling of restlessness, irritability, or boredom that occurs when a person is stuck indoors for an extended period.
5. **Chakras:** Energy centres in the body, corresponding to different physical, emotional, and spiritual aspects of a person's being. There are seven main chakras in a line along a person's spine: the root chakra, sacral chakra, solar plexus chakra, heart chakra, throat chakra, third eye chakra, and crown chakra.
6. **Consciousness:** The state of being aware of one's surroundings, thoughts, and feelings. It involves actively recognising and comprehending the state of existence.
7. **Divine Spirit:** A spiritual concept that refers to the inner essence of a person that is pure, perfect, and divine.
8. **Emotions:** Complex psychological states that involve a mix of chemicals and hormones the brain makes to create physiological stimuli. Emotions are fundamental to the human experience, influencing thoughts, behaviours, and overall well-being.
9. **Energy:** The force that sustains and animates all living things and is believed to exist in different forms and frequencies.

10. **Essence:** The fundamental nature or intrinsic quality of something.

11. **Hanuman:** A Hindu deity considered a symbol of strength, devotion, and loyalty.

12. **Innate Wisdom:** The intuitive and natural understanding a person has about themselves and the world around them.

13. **Intuition:** The ability to know or understand something without needing conscious reasoning or proof. An impression or insight gained by this faculty.

14. **Introspection:** The examination of one's thoughts and feelings.

15. **Meditation:** A practice or mental exercise in which an individual focuses on a particular object, thought, or activity to achieve a mentally clear and emotionally calm state and become aware of one's thoughts and feelings.

16. **Metaphysical:** Refers to concepts or ideas beyond the physical world or empirical reality.

17. **Mindful Eating:** A practice of paying attention to the present moment while eating, chewing food well, enjoying the flavours in each bite, and appreciating the blessings of life.

18. **Mindfulness**: A state of active, open attention to the present moment without judgment or distraction.

19. **Pineal Gland:** A small endocrine gland in the brain that produces and regulates hormones, including melatonin, associated with spiritual and mystical experiences.

20. **Salivary Glands:** Three kinds of glands in different areas of the mouth that squirt saliva when needed.

21. **Seeds of Knowledge:** When nurtured, small pieces of information or insight can grow and expand into more profound understanding.

22. **Self-love:** Honouring one's needs. Showing oneself compassion and appreciation, setting boundaries and being able to say "no" or "yes."

23. **Zen Moment:** A state of mind in which a person becomes fully absorbed in the present moment, letting go of past and future concerns and achieving a sense of inner peace and clarity.

Palachinta Recipe (spelled "palacsinta" in Hungarian)

Curious to taste the delicious dessert that Grandma Suzan made Ethan and the kids in the story? Here it is! Make these special Hungarian crepes yourself and share them with your loved ones.

These pancakes are large in diameter and very thin, unlike their North American cousins which are smaller in diameter yet thick.

The thin size of Hungarian crepes enables you to spread jam, cottage cheese, chocolate, nuts, or other foods on the crepe, and then roll it up for eating. You can also pour maple syrup, freshly made chocolate sauce, or other treats onto the rolled-up crepes.

Equipment:

- Mixing bowls
- Measuring cups
- Whisk
- Non-stick frying pan
- Spatula
- Fork
- Ladle
- Plates

Ingredients:

Batter
- 2 whole eggs
- 1 1/4 cups all-purpose flour
- 1 1/4 cups almond, oat, or other milk
- 2/3 cup sparkling water
- 1 pinch salt
- 1 teaspoon sugar
- Oil/fat for frying

Cottage cheese filling:
- 1 egg yolk
- 2/3 cup dry cottage cheese or ricotta
- 1/2 lemon zest
- 1 teaspoon vanilla extract
- 1 tablespoon sugar
- Mix, spread on crepe, roll up, and eat.

Walnut filling:
- Ground walnuts
- Sugar
- 2:1 ratio of walnuts to sugar (some people prefer a 1:1 ratio, adjust to your preference)

Instructions:

- Mix all ingredients except the
  sparkling water. Ensure there
  are no lumps in the batter.

- When smooth, add the
  sparkling water and mix.

- The consistency should be
  similar to that of a yogurt drink.
  Not too runny yet not thick.

- Set a frying pan over medium heat.
  Add a few drops of oil. Once hot, fill the
  ladle with batter and pour it evenly onto the
  frying pan.

- Tilt the pan in all directions so the batter coats the surface of the pan
  completely. If you have holes in the palachinta, fill them with a little batter.

- Fry the underside of the palachinta until it is a light golden brown colour.
  Use a spatula to loosen it from the frying pan and check the underside to
  be sure it is a golden colour.

- Flip the pancake and fry the other side as well. When done, slide the crepe
  onto a plate and prepare the pan for the next ladle of batter.

- Stir the mixture each time before pouring it into the pan.

- Repeat until you have used up all the batter.

- Spread each pancake with jam, walnut filling, or cottage cheese filling.
  Roll up and enjoy eating with friends and family.

The Mystic's Library of Excellence

The Mystic's Library of Excellence is a treasure trove (organized topic-wise) for those seeking to dive deeper into the ideas explored in the "Ethan and the Seven Chakras" books.

Topics include sacred geometry, remote viewing, near-death experiences, longevity practices, divine feminine and divine masculine concepts, championship mindsets, epigenetics, practical metaphysics, natural health practices, parthenogenesis, quantum physics, shamanism, energy medicine, ESP, and finance smarts.

For a detailed list with links, visit: www.singingsoulbooks.com

Each topic is a gateway to understanding the profound and the extraordinary. May your exploration be edifying and enriching.

Mind and Practical Metaphysics:

1. **Dr. Joe Dispenza**

    • **Books:** *Breaking the Habit of Being Yourself, Becoming Supernatural* (and other books)

    • Dispenza's work focuses on neuroscience, epigenetics, and quantum physics. His programs, books, and retreats guide people to elevate beyond their old patterns and create new ones toward a healthy, happy life.

2. **José Silva**

    • **Book:** *The Silva Method*

    • Silva's landmark work uses hypnosis and mental training to awaken the human mind's hidden potential beyond the traditional five senses.

3. **Florence Scovel Shinn**

    • **Books:** *The Game of Life and How to Play It, Your Word is Your Wand, The Secret Door to Success, The Power of the Spoken Word*

    • Emphasises the power of positive thought, affirmations, and spiritual principles for success and fulfilment.

4. **Esther and Jerry Hicks**

• **Books:** *Ask and It Is Given: Learning to Manifest Your Desires, The Astonishing Power of Emotions: Let Your Feelings Be Your Guide* (and other books)

• Explores the law of attraction and provides practical guidance on manifesting desires.

5. **Zinovia Dushkova**

• **Book:** *The Secret Book of Dzyan: Unveiling the Truth About the Oldest Manuscript in the World, Revelations of the Sun, The Teachings of the Heart* (and other books)

• Renowned author and philosopher, Zinovia Dushkova, Ph.D., was named one of the "100 Most Spiritually Influential Living People in 2020" by Watkins Mind Body Spirit magazine. She has written over 60 books, inspiring readers with her profound insights into love, compassion, and spiritual transformation.

6. **Neville Goddard**

• **Books:** *The Power of Imagination*

• Goddard's work delves into the transformative power of imagination and how it shapes our reality.

7. **Joseph Murphy**

• **Books:** *The Power of Your Subconscious Mind*

• Murphy explores how the subconscious mind influences behaviour and offers techniques to harness its power for personal success.

8. **Napoleon Hill**

• **Books:** *The Law of Success in Sixteen Lessons, Think and Grow Rich* (and other books)

• A classic in personal development, Hill's book outlines principles for achieving success and wealth through positive thinking and goal-setting.

9. **Dale Carnegie**

• **Books:** *How to Win Friends and Influence People*

• Carnegie provides timeless advice on effective communication, building relationships, and influencing others positively.

10. **David J. Schwartz**

   • **Books:** *The Magic of Thinking Big*

   • Schwartz encourages thinking beyond conventional limits to achieve personal and professional success.

11. **Maxwell Maltz**

   • **Books:** *Psycho-cybernetics*

   • Maltz explores the connection between self-image, success, and creativity.

12. **Claude M. Bristol**

   • **Books:** *The Magic of Believing*

   • Bristol explores the power of belief and how it can shape one's destiny.

13. **Peter B. Kyne**

   • **Books:** *The Go-Getter*

   • Kyne's book imparts valuable lessons on determination and achieving goals.

14. **RHJ**

   • **Books:** *It Works: The Little Red Book*

   • A concise guide to the power of positive thinking and manifestation.

15. **Russell H. Conwell**

   • **Books:** *Acres of Diamonds*

   • Conwell's book emphasises finding opportunities in one's own environment and recognizing the value of what is already at hand.

16. **James Allen**

   • **Books:** *As a Man Thinketh*

   • Allen's classic explores the impact of thoughts on character and circumstances, emphasising personal responsibility.

17. **Zig Ziglar**

   • **Books:** *See You At The Top*

   • Ziglar's teachings focus on motivation, goal-setting, and achieving success with a positive mindset.

18. **David Sereda**

   • **Private Membership Group:** *The Inner Circle*

   • David Sereda offers a community, products, and programs for those seeking personal and spiritual growth.

19. **Shahiroz Walji**

   • **Metaphysical Hub**

   • Shahiroz Walji's Metaphysical Hub provides resources and community for exploring metaphysical concepts.

20. **Proctor Gallagher Institute**

   • The Proctor Gallagher Institute focuses on personal development, prosperity, and transforming paradigms for success.

21. **Marisa Peer**

   • Marisa Peer is a renowned hypnotherapist and speaker, offering insights into transformation and mental well-being. Particularly known for her work in overcoming feelings of not being enough.

22. **Paul McKenna**

   • Paul McKenna provides resources for personal development and self-improvement through hypnosis and neuro-linguistic programming.

Consciousness, Quantum Physics, and Epigenetics:

1. **David R. Hawkins**

   • **Books:** *Map of Consciousness, Power Vs. Force* (and other books)

   • Hawkins explores the levels of human consciousness with a map to understand spiritual growth.

2. **Bruce H. Lipton, Ph.D.**

   • **Books:** *The Biology Of Belief, The Honeymoon Effect, Spontaneous Evolution*

   • Lipton's work bridges biology and spirituality, exploring how beliefs shape biology and influence health (epigenetics).

3. **Jacob Liberman**

  • **Books:** *Take Off Your Glasses and See: A Mind/Body Approach to Expanding Your Eyesight and Insight, Light: Medicine of the Future* (and other books)

  • Liberman combines a mind/body approach to vision, linking eyesight to broader insights and consciousness.

4. **Dr. Valerie V. Hunt**

  • **Books + DVDs:** *Infinite Mind: Science of the Human Vibrations of Consciousness, Uncork Your Consciousness* (and other books and DVDs)

  • Dr. Hunt delves into the science of human vibrations and their connection to consciousness.

5. **Dr. Konstantin Korotkov**

  • **Books:** *The Energy of Consciousness, Light After Life: Experiments and Ideas on After-Death Changes of Kirlian Pictures* (and other books)

  • Korotkov explores the scientific aspects of human energy fields and their relationship to consciousness.

6. **Dr. Joe Dispenza**

  • **Books:** *Becoming Supernatural, Breaking the Habit of Being Yourself*
  (and other books)

  • Dr. Joe Dispenza's work (books, courses, retreats) explores epigenetics.

7. **Gary Zukav**

  • **Books:** *Dancing Wu Li Masters: An Overview of the New Physics, The Seat of the Soul* (and other books)

  • Zukav explores the new physics, bridging science and spirituality.

8. **Fritjof Capra**

  • **Books:** *The Tao of Physics, The Turning Point* (and other books)

  • Capra explores parallels between modern physics and Eastern mysticism, highlighting the interconnectedness of science and spirituality.

ESP, Remote Viewing, Quantum Physics, and Consciousness Expansion:

1. Paul H. Smith

- **Book:** *The Essential Guide to Remote Viewing*

- Former CIA remote viewing trainer; offers programs in remote viewing and related skills. Smith is the longest serving Controlled Remote Viewing teacher from the US Army's Star Gate program.

2. Russell Targ

- **Books:** *Do You See What I See, The Reality of ESP* (and other books)

- Remote viewing and ESP. Targ is a physicist and researcher in remote viewing and extrasensory perception (ESP).

3. Ingo Swann

- **Books:** *Natural ESP, Preserving the Natural Child, Psychic Sexuality* (and other books)

- A researcher of the exceptional powers of the human mind and a leading figure in governmental and scientific projects to investigate and identify the scope of subtle human perceptions.

4. Dr. Dean Radin

- **Books:** *Real Magic, The Conscious Universe* (and other books)

- Explores psychic phenomena from a scientific lens.

5. ICU Academy

- ICU Academy provides training in remote viewing and psychic abilities.

6. Mark Komissarov and Mihaela Istrati

- Teaches InfoVision, a method for developing and utilising extrasensory perception.

7. The Monroe Institute

- The Monroe Institute provides programs focused on consciousness exploration through cutting-edge audio technology and immersive retreats.

8. **The Institute of Noetic Sciences**

> • Using science to explain phenomena not previously understood and harness the best of the mind to enhance human experience.

9. **The Parapsychological Association**

> • A professional organisation of scientists and scholars engaged in the study of 'psi' (or 'psychic') experiences, such as telepathy, clairvoyance, remote viewing, psychokinesis, psychic healing, and precognition.

10. **Dr. Fritz-Albert Popp**

> • Dr. Popp's research focuses on biophysics, particularly in biophotonics.

11. **Dan Winter**

> • Winter researches the physics of mystical experiences, gravitational energy, emotions, the evolution of consciousness, sacred geometry, quantum physics, and biofeedback.

12. **Dr. Fred Alan Wolf**

> • Wolf, a physicist and author, extensively explores the connections between quantum physics and consciousness.

13. **Dr. John Hagelin**

> • Hagelin's a quantum physicist whose research focuses on the role of consciousness in the universe and the potential of meditation to influence physical reality.

14. **Bruce Lipton**

> • **Books:** *The Biology of Belief, The Honeymoon Effect, Spontaneous Evolution*

> • Lipton, a cellular biologist and author, explores the connections between consciousness and biology, particularly in the science of epigenetics.

15. **Gregg Braden**

> • **Books:** *The God Code, The Divine Matrix, The Spontaneous Healing of Belief* (and other books)

> • Braden, a scientist and author, explores the science of consciousness and the impact of human emotion on physical reality.

1. Harold Klemp

- **Books:** *The Art of Spiritual Dreaming, ECK Wisdom on Karma and Reincarnation, Past Lives, Dreams, and Soul Travel* (and other books)

- Eckankar teaches techniques to explore one's inner worlds, including past lives, dreams, and Soul Travel.

2. Dr. Michael Newton

- **Book:** *Journey of Souls* (and other books)

- Explores the experiences of souls between lives. Through deep hypnosis sessions, Dr. Newton discovered that individuals could recall their existence as eternal spirits and describe their activities in the spirit world.

3. Dannion Brinkley

- **Books:** *10 Things to Know Before You Go, Saved by the Light* (and other books)

- Brinkley shares insights gained from his near-death experiences, providing wisdom on life and the afterlife.

4. Brian L. Weiss

- **Books:** *Through Time Into Healing, Same Soul, Many Bodies* (and other books)

- Weiss explores past lives and healing through regression therapy, emphasising the impact of past experiences on the present.

5. Raymond A. Moody Jr.

- **Books:** *The Light Beyond, Life After Life: The Investigation of a Phenomenon - Survival of Bodily Death* (and other books)

- Moody explores near-death experiences, shedding light on the transformative and spiritual aspects of these encounters.

6. NDE Stories

- A web compendium of near death experiences and resources from around the world. www.nderf.org

Parthenogenesis and the Divine Feminine:

1. **Marguerite Mary Rigoglioso**

- **Books:** *The Mystery Tradition of Miraculous Conception* (and other books)
- Rigoglios's courses and books explore the concept of miraculous conception, particularly in the context of the divine feminine lineage.

2. **Sri Sai Kaleshwara Swami**

- **Books:** *The Holy Womb; The Secrets of the Divine Mother's Creation* (and other books)
- Sri Sai Kaleshwara Swami dives into the sacredness of the feminine.

3. **Den Poitras**

- **Book: Parthenogenesis:** *Women's Long-Lost Ability to Self-Conceive*
- Poitras explores the concept of parthenogenesis, the ability to self-conceive.

4. **Jessie E. Ayani**

- **Books:** *The Lineage of the Codes of Light, The Priestess and Magus Trilogy* (and other books)
- Ayani explores the codes of light within the feminine lineage, emphasising spiritual and transformative aspects, to awaken the gifts within ourselves.

5. **Maureen Walton**

- **Book:** *The Good Darkness*
- Walton's work reveals a hidden female creation technology called the "Blood Masteries" that activate a woman's magnetic toroidal systems. This can help a woman elevate to a superconscious level.

6. **Kaia Ra**

- **Book:** *The Sophia Code*
- Ra's book and programs are a divine feminine, modern sacred text. It is considered a living transmission that aims to activate spiritual evolution and awakening, reminding us of how precious we are.

7. **Margaret Starbird**

> • **Book:** *The Woman with the Alabaster Jar*
>
> • Starbird explores the figure of Mary Magdalene and the symbolism of the Holy Grail in relation to the divine feminine.

8. **Tom Kenyon and Judi Sion**

> • **Book:** *Magdalen Manuscript*
>
> • Kenyon and Sion delve into the alchemies of Horus and the sex magic of Isis, exploring sacred feminine mysteries.

9. **Elizabeth Seraphine**

> • **Program:** *The Priestess Path Lineages of Light Mystery School*
>
> • Seraphine offers resources and teachings on the priestess path and the divine feminine, supporting women to embody their priestess mantle and express their true power.

10. **The Lemurian Sisterhood and Shamanic Teaching Wheel**

> • **Program:** The Lemurian Sisterhood and Shamanic Teaching Wheel explores concepts related to the divine feminine.

11. **Seven Sisters Mystery School**

> • The Seven Sisters Mystery School offers teachings and practices related to the mysteries of the divine feminine that help restore the ancient way of the Priestess.

12. **Alison A. Armstrong**

> • **Books:** *The Queen's Code* (and other books)
>
> • Armstrong's books and programs explore the biological reasons behind the behaviour of women and help decode them.

13. **RC Blakes Jr.**

> • **Books:** *Queenology*, (and other books)
>
> • **Website:** Offers insights for reigning as a queen in spite of the odds, for reclaiming self-esteem, and having the courage to step into your true power.

The Alpha Male and Divine Masculine:

1. **Alison A. Armstrong**

- **Books:** *The Amazing Development of Men* (and other books)

- Armstrong's books and programs explore the journey of men from knights to princes to kings, providing insights into male development.

2. **RC Blakes Jr.**

- **Books:** *Kingology: The Return of the King* (and other books)

- RC Blakes Jr. delves into Kingology, guiding men on the path of returning to their true kingly nature.

3. **Robert Moore and Douglas Gillette**

- **Books:** *King, Warrior, Magician, Lover* (and other books)

- Moore and Gillette explore the archetypes of the mature masculine, emphasising psychological development.

4. **Robert Bly**

- **Book:** *Iron John: A Book About Men*

- Bly delves into the mythopoetic men's movement, exploring the journey to mature masculinity.

5. **Brett and Kate McKay**

- **Book:** *The Art of Manliness*

- The McKay's book and magazine offer classic skills and manners for the modern man, emphasising the traditional masculine virtues of a gentleman.

6. **David Deida**

- **Book:** *The Way of the Superior Man*

- Deida's book and program addresses the complexities of sexual and spiritual evolution in today's fast-paced world.

7. **Men Without Masks**

- Men Without Masks is a program for men to explore authentic masculinity through various resources and community.

Communication Styles of Men and Women:

1. Alison A. Armstrong

- **Books:** *The Queen's Code, Making Sense of Men* (and other books)

- Armstrong explores the reasons behind the behaviour of men and women, and fundamental differences in how we think, act, and communicate.

2. RC Blakes Jr.

- **Books:** *The Father-Daughter Talk* (and other books)

- Blakes guides men and women to embrace their inherent value and power.

3. Gary Chapman

- **Book:** *The 5 Love Languages*

- Chapman's book identifies different love languages, helping individuals understand and communicate love more effectively.

4. John Gray

- **Books:** *What Your Mother Couldn't Tell You and Your Father Didn't Know, Men are From Mars and Women are From Venus* (and other books)

- Gray's books and courses offer advanced relationship skills providing practical guidance for improving communication, and understanding the differences between men and women.

5. Esther Perel

- **Books:** *Mating in Captivity*

- Perel's work explores the complexities of maintaining intimacy in long-term relationships and the role of communication in erotic intelligence.

6. Bibi Brzozka

- Brzozka focuses on female orgasmic potential and fostering deeper intimacy through effective communication.

7. Jaiya

- Jaiya's Erotic Blueprints provide a framework for empowered sexual communication, erotic ecstasy, and enhanced understanding between partners.

Taoism and Inner Alchemy:

1. Lao-Tzu

- **Book:** *Tao Te Ching*

- A classical Chinese text and foundational work of Taoism written around 400 BC and credited to the sage Laozi. In eighty-one chapters, Lao-tzu's Tao Te Ching, or Book of the Way, provides imparts advice on balance and perspective, a serene and generous spirit, and how to work for the good with the effortless skill that comes from being in accord with the Tao—the basic principle of the universe.

2. Daniel Reid

- **Book:** *The Tao of Health, Sex & Longevity* (and other books)

- Reid explores Taoist principles related to health, sex, and longevity, including the connection between inner alchemy and well-being.

3. Dr. Stephen Chang

- **Books:** *The Tao of Sexology, The Great Tao* (and other books)

- Chang's work delves into the Taoist perspective on sexology, using sexual techniques to enhance health, and Taoism; emphasising inner alchemy and its transformative effects on body and mind.

4. Dr. Felice Dunas

- **Book:** *Passion Play* (and other books)

- Dunas's books and courses incorporate powerful Taoist principles to improve health, sex, and intimacy, rectifying sexual dissatisfaction.

5. Mantak & Maneewan Chia

- **Books:** *Healing Love through the Tao: Cultivating Male Sexual Energy, The Multi-Orgasmic Couple* (and other books)

- The Chia's books and courses focus on cultivating male and female sexual energy, sexual secrets for couples, and enhanced intimacy through Taoist practices. These include learning to separate orgasm and ejaculation and retention practices for longevity and vitality, leading to multiple orgasm potential.

6. **Mantak Chia and Douglas Abrams**

   • **Book:** *The Multi-Orgasmic Man*

   • This collaborative work provides insights into sexual secrets every man should know, rooted in Taoist principles. These include learning to separate orgasm and ejaculation and retention practices for longevity and vitality, leading to multiple orgasm potential.

7. **Bruce Frantzis**

   • **Book:** *Taoist Sexual Meditation* (and other books)

   • Frantzis explores the connection between love, energy, and spirit through Taoist sexual meditation, emphasising communication within intimate relationships.

8. **Richard Wilhelm**

   • **Book:** *The Secret of the Golden Flower: A Chinese Book of Life*

   • The translation of this classic work explores the teachings of Taoism, including inner alchemy and the transformative journey of life. The language is flowery and sounds poetic, yet within lie many pearls of wisdom.

9. **Hsi Lai**

   • **Book:** *The Sexual Teachings of the White Tigress: Secrets of the Female Taoist Masters* (and other books)

   • Lai delves into the teachings of female Taoist masters within the context of sexual and spiritual wisdom.

10. **Thomas Cleary**

   • **Book:** *The Taoist Classics, Volume 1* (and other books)

   • Cleary's translations provide access to essential Taoist texts, offering insights into inner alchemy and Taoist philosophy.

11. **John Heider**

   • **Books:** *The Tao of Leadership, The Tao of Daily Living*

   • Heider applies Taoist principles to leadership, emphasising effective communication and harmony in relationships.

12. **Eva Wong**

   • **Books:** Taoism: *An Essential Guide, Cultivating Stillness: A Taoist Manual for Transforming Body and Mind* (and other books)

   • Wong's books provide an overview of Taoism, including its principles of inner alchemy and communication.

13. **Robert Lawlor**

   • **Book:** *Earth Honoring: The New Male Sexuality* (and other books)

   • Lawlor explores sexual behaviour in ancient traditions like Tantra and Taoism, offering insights into redirecting male energy from excess to constructive paths. He details specific techniques used in sexual and spiritual training to harness creative potential and spiritual growth.

Martial Arts Philosophy:

1. **Patrick McCarthy**

   • **Book:** *The Bubishi*

   • Treasured for centuries by top martial arts masters, the Bubishi is a classic Chinese work on philosophy, strategy, medicine, and technique as they relate to the martial arts. For hundreds of years, the Bubishi was a secret text passed from master to student in China and later in Okinawa. No other classic work has had as dramatic an impact on the shaping and development of karate as the Bubishi. Karate historian and authority Patrick McCarthy spent over ten years researching and studying the Bubishi and the arts associated with it. His work includes groundbreaking research on Okinawan and Chinese history, as well as the fighting and healing traditions that developed in those countries, making it a gold mine for researchers and practitioners alike.

2. **Richard Kim**

   • **Book:** *The Classical Man* (and other books)

   • Kim's work explores martial arts philosophy, emphasising character development. This book shares the historically significant lives of real martial arts masters.

3. **Deng Ming-Dao**

   • **Book:** *Chronicles of the Tao: The Secret Life of a Taoist Master* (and other books)

• Ming-Dao's chronicles provide insights into the real life and wisdom of Taoist master, Kwan Saihung who was born into a wealthy martial arts family and became the thirteenth and last discipline of the grand master of the sacred mountain known as Huashan.

4. Chen Kaiguo, Zheng Shunchao, Thomas Cleary

• **Book:** *Opening the Dragon Gate: The Making of a Modern Taoist Wizard*

• The biography of Wang Liping, a modern Taoist wizard, is the true story of how a young boy becomes heir to a tradition of esoteric knowledge and practice through an arduous fifteen-year apprenticeship, learning the true source of health, healing, and long life.

5. Soke C. J. Rupert Juta

• **Book:** *Tao-Shukokairyu Odyssey* (and other books)

• Juta's work explores the martial arts style and philosophy of Tao-Shukokairyu, offering insights into the journey of a martial artist, focusing on mindset and critical thinking.

6. Gichin Funakoshi

• **Book:** *Karate-Do: My Way of Life*

• Funakoshi, known as the "Father of Karate-do," shares his journey from the secrecy of Okinawan self-defence to the global practice of martial arts. Funakoshi refined techniques and emphasised spirituality. Through anecdotes of his renowned teachers and personal trials, he unveils the essence of authentic karate and exemplifies principles of perseverance, self-reliance, and samurai ethos.

7. Bruce Lee

• **Book:** *The Tao of Jeet Kune Do*

• The book details the science and philosophy behind the fighting system Lee pioneered. It is the original mixed martial art known as Jeet Kune Do—"the way of the intercepting fist.

8. Miyamoto Musashi

• **Book:** *The Book of Five Rings*

• Musashi's classic work presents martial arts philosophy through the lens of strategy and the way of the samurai.

9. **Joe Hyams**

   • **Book:** *Zen in the Martial Arts*

   • Hyams reveals how the daily application of Zen principles developed his physical expertise and gave him the mental discipline to control his personal problems, and how understanding the spiritual goals in martial arts can dramatically alter the quality of your life.

10. **Forrest E. Morgan**

   • **Book:** *Living the Martial Way*

   • Morgan's book offers a step-by-step approach to applying the Japanese warrior's mindset to martial training and daily life.

11. **Sun Tzu**

   • **Book:** *The Art of War*

   • An ancient Chinese military treatise composed of 13 chapters and attributed to the military strategist Sun Tzu. It explores skills dedicated to warfare and how it applies to military strategy and tactics including psychology.

Shamanism and Psychedelic Plants:

1. **Mircea Eliade**

   • **Book:** *Shamanism: Archaic Techniques of Ecstasy* (and other books)

   • Eliade surveys the tradition of shamanism (at once magicians and medicine men and women, healers and miracle-doers, priests, mystics, and poets) through two and a half millennia of human history, illuminating the magico-religious life of societies.

2. **Michael Harner**

   • **Book:** *The Way of the Shaman* (and other books)

   • Harner's book introduces core shamanic practices and principles, shedding light on the role of shamans in different societies, what it is, where it came from, and how you can participate.

3. **Lynn Andrews**

   • **Book:** *The Medicine Woman book series* (and other books)

   • Andrews' books, programs, and mystery school offer training into modern-day shamanism and the divine feminine, offering insights into healing and wisdom.

4. **Andrew Weil**

- **Books:** *The Natural Mind, The Marriage of the Sun and Moon* (and other books)

- In The Natural Mind, Weil suggests that the desire to alter consciousness periodically is an innate, normal human drive. In The Marriage of the Sun and the Moon, he examines the integration of masculine and feminine energies, drawing inspiration from shamanic experiences.

5. **Carlos Castaneda**

- **Book:** *The Teachings of Don Juan: A Yaqui Way of Knowledge* (and other books)

- Castaneda's books recount Don Juan's apprenticeship with a Yaqui Indian shaman, exploring shamanic teachings and a new way of seeing the world.

6. **Eliot Cowan**

- **Book:** *Plant Spirit Medicine*

- Cowan's book explores the healing potential of plant spirits, connecting shamanic principles with the medicinal properties of plants.

7. **Jeremy Narby**

- **Book:** *The Cosmic Serpent: DNA and the Origins of Knowledge*

- Narby investigates the connection between shamanic knowledge and DNA, exploring the mysteries of consciousness and evolution.

Health (Wholeness) and Healing:

1. **Dr. Bradley Nelson**

- **Books:** *The Emotion Code, The Body Code*

- Nelson's books and work focuses on techniques that release trapped emotions to ease physical and emotional ailments.

2. **Dr. Ryke Geerd Hamer**

- **Book:** *Summary of the New Medicine*

- Hamer's work presents a very different approach to understanding cancer, how diseases develop, and the mind-body connection. His research led him to believe that diseases are a result of biological conflict, shock, or trauma (if not a result of poison or an injury). He discovered that each biological conflict leaves a visible mark in the brain (confirmed by a CT scan) and that the nature of the conflict predetermined the site of the disease. The result of his research was the creation of a disease chart that accurately describes the biological conflict cause of each disease, the exact location in the brain where the focus is found, and how the disease manifests during the conflict active phase and resolution phases.

3. David R. Hawkins

• **Books:** *The Spectrum of Consciousness Explained: A Proven Energy Scale to Actualize Your Ultimate Potential, Power Vs. Force, Healing and Recovery* (and other books)

• Hawkins' work explores healing and recovery from a spiritual perspective, integrating consciousness and health. He developed a map that defines a range of values, attitudes, and emotions that correspond to levels of consciousness and provides practical applications to help people heal and evolve to higher levels of consciousness and energy. He posits that an individual's power and level of consciousness can be enhanced through greater integrity, understanding, and compassion.

4. Lars Muhl

• **Book:** *The Gate of Light: Healing Practices to Connect You to Source Energy* (and other books)

• Muhl's book is an introduction to the long-forgotten healing methods of the Essenes, and offers useful tools, meditations, and visualisations for modern-day practitioners.

5. Deepak Chopra

• **Book:** *Quantum Healing: Exploring the Frontiers of Mind/Body Medicine* (and other books)

• Chopra's work combines Western medicine, neuroscience, and physics with the insights of Ayurvedic theory to show that the human body is controlled by a "network of intelligence" grounded in quantum reality. Not a superficial psychological state, this intelligence lies deep enough to change the basic patterns that design our physiology, with the potential to overcome illness.

6. Michael Breus

• **Book:** *The Power of When*

• Breus's work on the science of sleep presents a groundbreaking program for getting back in sync with your natural rhythm (chronobiology) by making minor changes to your daily routine. Working with your body's inner clock for maximum health, happiness, and productivity becomes easy and fun.

7. Felice Dunas

- **Book:** *Passion Play* (and other books)

- Dunas's books and courses focus on healing through pleasure; incorporating powerful Taoist principles to improve health, sex, and intimacy, leading to more meaningful connections and a more satisfying life.

8. Nadia Volf

- **Book:** *Mysteries of the Ear: Secrets of Well-Being*

- Volf is the creator of the Auricular Causative Diagnostic method. Her work reveals the extraordinary powers of the auricular (ear) acupuncture points, making it possible to provide relief for everyday ailments.

9. Konstantin Sukhov

- **Book:** *Clinical Hirudotherapy: Practical Guide: Book 1. General Hirudotherapy* (and other books)

- Sukhov's guide explores the therapeutic use of medicinal leeches, known as hirudotherapy, to address a wide array of health complaints.

10. HP Ekkehard Scheller

- **Book:** *Candidalism*

- Scheller's work examines the impact of candida overgrowth on health and well-being, contributing to the understanding of candidalism. Borrelias, viruses, and other pathogens have learned to camouflage themselves to keep from being attacked by our immune system and strong drugs. Thanks to Dark Field Microscopy of blood and Radionic Testing, Ekkehard Sirian Scheller discovered the camouflaged Candida fungi, which varied their shape to keep from being detected. Due to the fermentation of glucose, extreme mycotoxins are produced, which destroy the mucosal system due to constant corrosion. As a result, many secondary diseases arise.

11. Artour Rakhimov

- **Book:** *Breathing Slower and Less: The Greatest Health Discovery Ever* (Buteyko Method) (and other books)

• Rakhimov's book explores the health benefits of the buteyko breathing method and its impact on well-being. Learn how breathing retraining can prevent and alleviate many diseases, along with insights from clinical trials, lifestyle factors, and breathing retraining techniques. Embark on a journey to long-term health and vitality.

12. **James Nestor**

• **Book: Breath:** *The New Science of a Lost Art*

• Nestor's exploration of breath delves into the science and art of breathing, emphasising its crucial role in health.

13. **Ben Greenfield**

• **Book:** *Boundless: Upgrade Your Brain, Optimize Your Body, & Defy Aging*

• Greenfield is a walking encyclopedia of biohacking wisdom, blending cutting-edge science with practical tips for a vibrant life. As a health consultant, speaker, and author, he aims to optimise life for boundless energy and fulfilment through his books, podcasts and coaching. He specialises in longevity, anti-aging, biohacking, and positive psychology.

14. **Dr. Gabor Maté**

• **Book:** *When the Body Says No: The Cost of Hidden Stress, The Myth of Normal: Trauma, Illness, and Healing in a Toxic Culture* (and other books)

• An addiction expert, Dr. Maté is the creator of the psychotherapeutic approach, Compassionate Inquiry. His books and work explore the connection between stress, emotions, and addiction and disease, offering insights into the mind-body connection.

15. **Bessel van der Kolk**

• **Book:** *The Body Keeps the Score: Brain, Mind, and Body in the Healing of Trauma*

• Van der Kolk's influential work explores the impact of trauma on the body and mind, offering approaches to healing.

16. **Dr. Anna Lembke**

• **Book:** *Dopamine Nation: Finding Balance in the Age of Indulgence*

• Lembke's book explores the role of dopamine in modern society and its impact on health, addiction, and well-being.

17. **Jonathon Aslay**

> • **Book:** *What The Heck Is Self-Love Anyway?*

> • Aslay's book and relationship coaching focus on self-love as a fundamental aspect of health and well-being, contributing to personal development and healthy relationships.

18. **Barbara Ann Brennan**

> • **Book:** *Hands of Light: A Guide to Healing Through the Human Energy Field* (and other books)

> • Brennan's book explores energy healing through the human energy field, offering insights into holistic health practices.

19. **Emily Matweow**

> • Emily Matweow is a master energy healer and medical intuitive specialising in energy healing, medical intuition, removing blocks, and empowering clients to regain balance, clarity, and peace.

20. **Alvin De Leon**

> • Dr. Alvin De Leon focuses on empowered health through the principles of Dr. Hamer's German New Medicine, based on the 5 biological laws.

21. **Brent Bruning**

> • **Book:** *The Power in Your Hands*

> • Bruning's work specialises in breaking through trauma patterns using biological blueprints as seen in the hands, offering innovative approaches to healing. Web: www.thepowerinyourhands.com

> • **Bonus for readers! Coupon Codes for:**
>> • A 2-hour Hand Analysis + Life Pattern Session
>> Coupon code: StoryMaster (receive $100 off)
>> • The Shift or The Hero's Journey program: Mastering your shadows to break through to your exalted Self
>> Coupon code: StorymasterProduct (receive $100 off)

22. **David Sereda**

> • David Sereda offers frequency-based healing products and programs, exploring the intersection of sound, vibrational alignment, and health.

23. Medical Medium Anthony William

- **Books:** *Brain Saver, Thyroid Healing, Medical Medium* (and other books)

- Medical Medium Anthony William was born with the unique ability to converse with the Spirit of Compassion, who provides him with extraordinarily advanced healing information far ahead of its time. He is considered a chronic illness expert and is the originator of the global celery juice movement and Brain Shot Therapy.

24. Vibrational Revelations with Elena Bensenoff and Alejandro Ferradas

- Using integrative and quantum medicine, paired with vibrational frequency measurements of your level of consciousness (based on the work of David R. Hawkins's map of consciousness), Elena Bensenoff and Alejandro Ferradas offer resources on vibrational healing and frequency readings for clients.

25. Bio-resonance Life Flow: Health Scans & Consultations with Yvette Farkas

- Get a clear picture of your health with a bio-resonance scan. It tests for viruses, bacteria, mold, parasites, allergies, food intolerances, heavy metals, inflammation, and more. Even the strength of the auric field is shown. Detailed health scans provide insights into energetic imbalances and blocks to health, empowering you to make more informed decisions to increase vitality, wellbeing, and energy. Web: www.bioresonancescans.com

26. Thich Nhat Hanh: International Plum Village Community

- Thich Nhat Hanh is a Zen master, the founder of Plum Village, numerous movements and charities, and the author of over 100 books focusing on mindfulness.

27. HeartMath Institute

- The HeartMath Institute explores the connection between heart health, emotions, and overall well-being, offering practical tools for self-regulation.

28. Bryan Johnson

- Bryan Johnson's biohacking protocol focuses on health optimization, contributing to personalised approaches to wellbeing.

29. Edgar Cayce's Association for Research and Enlightenment (A.R.E.)

- **Book:** *The Essential Edgar Cayce* (and other books)

• The Association for Research and Enlightenment (A.R.E.) offers body-mind-spirit resources and educational programs that foster personal transformation through the wisdom embedded in the extensive collection of Edgar Cayce's readings. Edgar Cayce is a twentieth-century seer and intuitive healer. The book features Cayce's most intriguing and influential readings, and a biographical introduction to his life.

30. Diagnostic Testing of One's Biological Age

• TruDiagnostic offers diagnostic testing of one's biological age, providing insights into overall health and longevity.

Yoga Philosophy:

1. Swami Sivananda

• **Books:** *Bliss Divine, Practice of Bhakti Yoga* (and other books)

• Swami Sivananda is the founder of the The Divine Life Society, the inspiration behind the Sivananda Yoga Vedanta Centres and Yasodhara ashrams, and the author of over 300 books.

2. Swami Sivananda Radha

• **Books:** *Mantras; Words of Power, Radha; Diary of a Woman's Search* (and other books)

• Swami Sivananda Radha is the founder of Canada's first ashram - Yasodhara Ashram, and opened the Yoga Vedanta bookstore.

3. Swami Vishnu-Devananda

• **Books:** *Meditation and Mantras, The Classical Illustrated Book of Yoga* (and other books)

• Swami Vishnu-Devananda founded the Sivananda Yoga Vedanta Centres and is the author of numerous books.

4. Swami Satchidananda

• **Books:** *The Yoga Sutras of Patanjali, Key to Peace* (and other books)

• Swami Satchidananda founded Integral Yoga International and Satchidananda Ashram - Yogaville and is the author of numerous books.

5. Swami Satyananda

- **Books:** *Asana, Pranayama, Mudra, and Bandha, Yoga Nidra* (and other books)

- Swami Satyananda founded International Yoga Fellowship Movement and The Bihar School of Yoga, and authored numerous books.

6. The Bhagavad Gita

- The Bhagavad Gita (Sanskrit: "Song of God") is a foundational text in yoga philosophy, offering profound teachings on duty, righteousness, and the path to spiritual realisation.

7. Sri Kaleshwar

- **Book:** *The Holy Womb - The Secrets of The Divine Mother's Creation: A Rendering of the Teachings of Sri Sai Kaleshwara Swami* (and other books)

- Kaleshwar's work delves into the mysteries of divine consciousness, contributing to the understanding of spirituality and self-realisation.

8. Yogacharya B.K.S.Iyengar

- **Book:** *Light on Yoga: The Bible of Modern Yoga* (and other books)

- B.K.S.Iyengar founded the Ramamani Iyengar Memorial Yoga Institute (RIMYI) and authored numerous books.

9. TKV Desikachar

- **Book:** *The Heart of Yoga: Developing a Personal Practice* (and other books)

- TKV Desikachar developed Viniyoga and founded the Krishnamacharya Yoga Mandiram (KYM), and has authored numerous books.

10. Sri Aurobindo + The Mother

- Sri Aurobindo is the author of several books and co-founder with The Mother of the Sri Aurobindo Ashram. In addition to spending 50 years overseeing the growth of this many-faceted spiritual community, The Mother established Sri Aurobindo International Centre of Education, and an international township called Auroville.

Ayurveda (The Science of Life):

1. Dr. Robert E. Svoboda

   • **Books:** *Ayurveda: Life, Health and Longevity, Prakriti: Your Ayurvedic Constitution* (and other books)

   • Dr. Robert Svoboda's books and programs provide a comprehensive overview of Ayurveda, exploring its principles and practices for maintaining health and longevity.

2. Dr. Vasant Dattatray Lad

   • **Books:** *Ayurveda: The Science of Self-Healing: A Practical Guide, The Complete Book of Ayurvedic Home Remedies* (and other books)

   • Dr. Vasant Lad is the founder of the Ayurvedic Institute and the author of 12 books. His work disseminates the timeless principles and practices of Ayurvedic - The Science of Life.

3. Dr. David Frawley and Dr. Vasant Dattatray Lad

   • **Book:** *The Yoga of Herbs: An Ayurvedic Guide to Herbal Medicine*

   • This collaborative work explores the intersection of Ayurveda and herbal medicine, offering insights into natural healing.

4. Dr. David Frawley

   • **Book:** *Ayurveda and the Mind: The Healing of Consciousness* (and other books)

   • Dr. David Frawley is the founder of The American Institute of Vedic Studies and author of several books exploring the rich knowledge of Ayurveda.

5. Maya Bri. Tiwari

   • **Book:** *Ayurveda: Secrets of Healing* (and other books)

   • Maya Tiwari is the founder of The Wise Earth School of Ayurveda and Mother Om Mission (MOM). Her books and work share the healing path of Ayurveda, unveiling its secrets for healing and maintaining balance.

6. Amadea Morningstar

   • **Book:** *The Ayurvedic Cookbook* (and other books)

   • Amadea Morningstar is the founder of the Ayurveda Polarity Therapy and Yoga Institute. She is an author, speaker, and Ayurvedic practitioner and instructor.

Sacred Geometry and Physics:

1. Gyorgy Doczi

- **Book:** *The Power of Limits: Proportional Harmonies in Nature, Art, and Architecture*

- Doczi explores the concept of proportional harmonies in various aspects of life, art, and architecture through sacred geometry.

2. Robert Lawlor

- **Book:** *Sacred Geometry: Philosophy and Practice* (and other books)

- Lawlor's work delves into the philosophical and practical aspects of sacred geometry, exploring its significance in diverse disciplines.

3. Matila Ghyka

- **Book:** *The Geometry of Art and Life*

- Ghyka's book connects geometry with art and life, revealing the inherent mathematical principles that underlie both.

4. Les Brown

- **Book:** *The Pyramid*

- This resource explores the use of pyramids for healing and meditation, offering insights into their potential benefits.

5. NOAA - Magnetic Field Calculators

- The NOAA website provides tools for calculating the Earth's magnetic field, including declination, useful for aligning pyramids with the Earth's magnetic forces.

6. David Sereda

- Sereda, a researcher and filmmaker, offers insights into UFOs, quantum physics, and spirituality, providing a deeper understanding of the universe and human potential.

7. David Wilcock

- Wilcock, a researcher and lecturer, explores the convergence of science and spirituality, investigating topics like UFOs, consciousness, and the universe's mysteries, often incorporating sacred geometry and metaphysical concepts.

1. **Ken Honda**

   • **Book:** *Happy Money: The Japanese Art of Making Peace with Your Money*

   (and other books)

   • Ken Honda explores the relationship between happiness and money, offering insights from Japanese philosophy to create a harmonious connection with finances.

2. **T. Harv Eker**

   • **Book:** *Secrets of the Millionaire Mind: Mastering the Inner Game of Wealth*

   • Eker delves into the mindset and psychological aspects that contribute to financial success, providing guidance on cultivating a wealthy mindset.

3. **Robert G. Allen**

   • **Book:** *Multiple Streams of Income: How to Generate a Lifetime of Unlimited Wealth!*

   • Allen introduces the concept of creating multiple income streams for long-term financial success, outlining strategies for generating wealth.

4. **Sam Rossi and Andra Pickens**

   • **Book:** *Quantum Networking: How to Play the Game that the Wealthiest and Happiest People Play... Starting Today*

   • Rossi and Pickens explore the principles of quantum networking, offering a unique perspective on building connections for financial success.

5. **George S. Clason**

   • **Book:** *The Richest Man in Babylon*

   • Clason's classic imparts timeless financial wisdom through parables set in ancient Babylon, addressing principles of wealth-building.

6. **Thomas J. Stanley and William D. Danko**

   • **Book:** *The Millionaire Next Door: The Surprising Secrets of America's Wealthy*

   • Stanley and Danko reveal common traits and habits of self-made millionaires, challenging stereotypes and offering practical insights for building wealth.

7. Napoleon Hill

- **Book:** *Think and Grow Rich*
- Hill's seminal work outlines principles for success and wealth, emphasising the power of mindset and goal-setting.

8. Morgan Housel

- **Book:** *The Psychology of Money: Timeless Lessons on Wealth, Greed, and Happiness*
- Housel explores the psychological aspects of money management, providing insights into the behaviours that influence financial decisions.

9. Alex Hormozi

- **Book:** *$100M Offers: How to Make Offers So Good People Feel Stupid Saying No*
- Hormozi shares strategies for crafting irresistible offers that create compelling opportunities for financial success.

10. Tony Robbins

- **Book:** *MONEY Master the Game: 7 Simple Steps to Financial Freedom* (and other books)
- Robbins' work provides practical steps for achieving financial and personal freedom to live your best life.

11. Robert & Kim Kiyosaki

- **Book:** *Rich Dad, Poor Dad: What the Rich Teach Their Kids About Money - That the Poor and Middle Class Do Not!* (and other books)
- The Kiyosaki's books, programs and games offer educational programs for financial freedom that are simple enough for a 9-year old to understand.

12. Bob Proctor

- **Book:** *You Were Born Rich*
- Proctor's teachings focus on unlocking one's innate potential for wealth and success, emphasising the abundance within each individual.

13. Ramit Sethi

- **Book:** *I Will Teach You to Be Rich*
- Sethi's book and courses provide practical advice on personal finance, covering topics such as saving, investing, and creating a rich life.

Behaviour and Body Language:

1. **Chris Voss**

- **Book:** *Never Split the Difference: Negotiating As If Your Life Depended On It*

- Voss, a former FBI negotiator, shares negotiation techniques and strategies, providing insights into effective communication and persuasion.

2. **Vanessa Van Edwards**

- **Book: Captivate:** *The Science of Succeeding with People*

- Van Edwards explores the science of interpersonal communication, offering practical tips and strategies for connecting with others.

3. **Joe Navarro**

- **Book:** *What Every Body is Saying*

- Navarro, a former FBI agent, decodes nonverbal communication, providing insights into reading body language for improved understanding and communication.

4. **Rebecca Zung**

- **Book:** *How to Negotiate with a Bully (Narcissist)*

- Zung provides guidance on negotiating with challenging personalities, particularly narcissists, offering strategies for effective communication.

5. **Ramani Durvasula, PhD**

- **Book:** *It's Not You*

- Dr. Durvasula explores relationships with narcissists, providing insights into understanding and navigating these challenging dynamics.

Transmitted and Channelled Information:

1. **Kryon**

- **Books:** *Don't Think Like a Human, The Twelve Layers of DNA, The Indigo Children, The Women of Lemuria* (and other books)

- Kryon offers channelled information via books, programs, and retreats, providing spiritual insights and teachings, contributing to personal and collective transformation.

2. Abraham Hicks

- **Books:** *Ask and It is Given: Learning to Manifest Your Desires, The Astonishing Power of Emotions* (and other books)
- Abraham Hicks, channelled by Esther Hicks, shares teachings on the law of attraction, manifestation, and spiritual guidance via books, programs, and retreats.

3. Law of One

- The Law of One provides channelled material offering perspectives on spirituality, the nature of reality, and the evolution of consciousness.

4. Ashayana Deane

- **Books:** *Voyagers: The Sleeping Abductees - Volume 1, Voyagers: The Secrets of Amenti - Volume 2* (and other books)
- Ashayana Deane's work explores ascension mechanics and multidimensional consciousness, providing insights into spiritual evolution.

5. Sarah Landon

- **Books:** *The Wisdom of the Council: Channelled Messages for Living Your Purpose, The Dream, The Journey, Eternity, And God: Channeled Answers to Life's Deepest Questions*
- Sarah Landon shares channelled information and spiritual teachings to assist individuals on their path of self-discovery and personal growth.

6. Emily Matweow

- **Book:** *INTUITION: Discover 11 Different Kinds* (and other books)
- Emily Matweow is a master energy healer and medical intuitive, providing insights and guidance for holistic well-being.

7. Lee Harris

- **Book:** *Conversations with the Z's*
- Harris is an energy intuitive, author, and musician. His grounded, practical teachings focus on the expansion of awareness to help you live a more heart-centred life.

1. MindValley

- MindValley offers personal development and education programs, focusing on holistic growth, consciousness, and well-being.

2. Regan Hillyer

- Regan Hillyer provides coaching and mentorship for individuals seeking personal and financial transformation, emphasising conscious leadership.

3. Juan Pa Barahona

- Juan Pa Barahona offers coaching and mentorship, guiding individuals towards personal and professional success through conscious leadership.

4. Marcel Szenessy

- Marcel Szenessy provides seminars and coaching, emphasising personal development and conscious leadership for individuals and organisations.

5. Yvette Farkas

- Yvette Farkas is a health-based coach and mentor, an author, and practitioner of ancient healing practices taking people back to their health and their hearts.

6. Daria Vodopianova

- Daria Vodopianova contributes to conscious leadership and mentorship, focusing on empowering individuals in their personal and professional journeys.

7. Tony Robbins

- Tony Robbins is a renowned life coach and motivational speaker, offering programs and events focused on personal development, wealth creation, and leadership.

8. Brent Bruning

- Brent Bruning's work specialises in breaking through trauma patterns using biological blueprints as seen in the hands, offering innovative approaches to healing through in-depth coaching and mentorship.

1. **David Wilcock**

- **Book:** *Awakening in the Dream:Contact with the Divine* (and other books)

- Wilcock explores topics related to consciousness, spirituality, and the nature of reality, providing insights into awakening and self-discovery.

2. **Jessie Ayani**

- **Book:** *The Brotherhood of the Magi* (and other books)

- Ayani's work explores mystical and esoteric themes, offering insights into ancient wisdom and the spiritual journey of the Magi.

3. **Vladimir Nikolaevich Megre**

- **Book: Anastasia:** *Ringing Cedars of Russia* (9 books)

- Megre's "Anastasia" series revolves around a Siberian recluse named Anastasia, sharing her wisdom on nature, spirituality, and the interconnectedness of all life.

4. **Michael A. Singer**

- **Book:** *The Surrender Experiment: My Journey into Life's Perfection* (and other books)

- Singer recounts his personal journey of surrendering to life's flow, providing a profound exploration of spiritual surrender and personal growth.

5. **Zecharia Sitchin**

- **Book:** *The Anunnaki Chronicles: A Zecharia Sitchin Reader* (and other books)

- Sitchin's collection delves into ancient Sumerian texts, offering interpretations and insights into the possible extraterrestrial influence on human history.

6. **Peter Ragnar**

- **Book:** *Finding Heart: How to Live with Courage in a Confusing World*

- Ragnar shares his perspective on courage and navigating life's challenges, providing insights and practical wisdom for personal development.

7. **Richard P. Feynman**

- **Book:** *Surely You're Joking, Mr. Feynman! Adventures of a Curious Character*

• Feynman's memoir offers humorous anecdotes and reflections on his life as a physicist, showcasing his curious and playful approach to understanding the world.

8. **Joseph Campbell**

• **Book:** *The Power of Myth* (and other books)

• Campbell explores the power of myth and its role in human culture, drawing connections between ancient stories and contemporary life.

9. **Dan Millman**

• **Book:** *Way of the Peaceful Warrior*

• Millman's novel combines fiction and autobiographical elements, conveying spiritual teachings through the story of a young athlete's journey toward enlightenment.

10. **Rudolf Steiner**

• **Book:** *Bees*

• Steiner delves into the spiritual significance of bees and their role in the natural world, offering insights into the interconnectedness of life.

11. **Jacqueline Freeman**

• **Book:** *Song of Increase: Returning to Our Sacred Relationship with Honeybees*

• Freeman explores the sacred relationship between humans and honeybees, emphasising the spiritual and ecological importance of these creatures.

12. **Richard Bach**

• **Book:** *Illusions: The Adventures of a Reluctant Messiah* (and other books)

• Bach's philosophical novel explores the nature of reality, illusion, and the potential for each individual to discover their divine nature.

13. **Hermann Hesse**

• **Book:** *Siddhartha*

• Hesse's novel follows the journey of Siddhartha, exploring themes of self-discovery, enlightenment, and the spiritual path.

14. **Robin Sharma**

   • **Book:** *The Monk Who Sold His Ferrari*

   • Sharma's book combines fiction and self-help, telling the story of a successful lawyer's spiritual journey toward a more meaningful and fulfilling life.

15. **Neale Donald Walsch**

   • **Books:** *Conversations With God: An Uncommon Dialogue (Books 1-3)*
   (and other books)

   • Walsch's book presents a dialogue with the divine, offering profound insights into spirituality and the soul's journey.

Devices for Health and Healing:

1. **David Sereda's Products (the largest frequency library in the world)**

   • Sereda offers a diverse range of products, including frequency libraries, designed to promote health and well-being through vibrational and energy principles. Web: www.davidsereda.co

2. **Safe Laser**

   • A new generation of lasers for therapeutic use. The Safe Laser family has analgesic and anti-inflammatory effects and speeds up healing and regeneration of the body. Web: www.safelaser.hu/en

3. **Jonathan Goldman's Chakra Chants Tuning Forks**

   • Goldman's tuning forks are designed to align with chakras, offering a sound-based approach to balancing and harmonising energy centres in the body

4. **Bio-Well**

   • Bio-Well is a device that measures and visualises the human energy field, providing insights into overall wellbeing and energy balance.
   Web: www.bio-well.store

5. **SomaVedic**

   • Products that utilise frequency therapy and natural science to harmonise spaces and water, and reduce the impact of harmful EMFs.
   Web: www.somavedic.com

The Most Important Things I Learned From This Book:

www.ingramcontent.com/pod-product-compliance
Lightning Source LLC
Chambersburg PA
CBHW041208100726
47911CB00017B/897